The Hunter

Michael Aye

BOOK THREE, THE PYRATE

Deadman's Bay

PYRATE
The Hunter

Book 3

Michael Aye

Published by Boson Books

An imprint of Bitingduck Press

Formerly an imprint of C&M Online Media, Inc.

ISBN 978-1-68553-010-5

eISBN 978-1-68553-006-8

For information contact

Bitingduck Press, LLC

Altadena, CA

notifications@bitingduckpress.com

http://www.bitingduckpress.com

Cover art by Mike Benton

Map of the Caribbean by Kmusser, under terms of the Creative Commons license; edited to fit pagination.

https://creativecommons.org/licenses/by-sa/3.0/

Author's note

This book is a work of fiction with a historical backdrop. I have taken liberties with historical figures, ships, and time frames to blend in with my story. Therefore, this book is not a reflection of actual historical events.

Books by Michael Aye

Dedication

Chris Duncklee – Master artist and boat builder, this one is for you

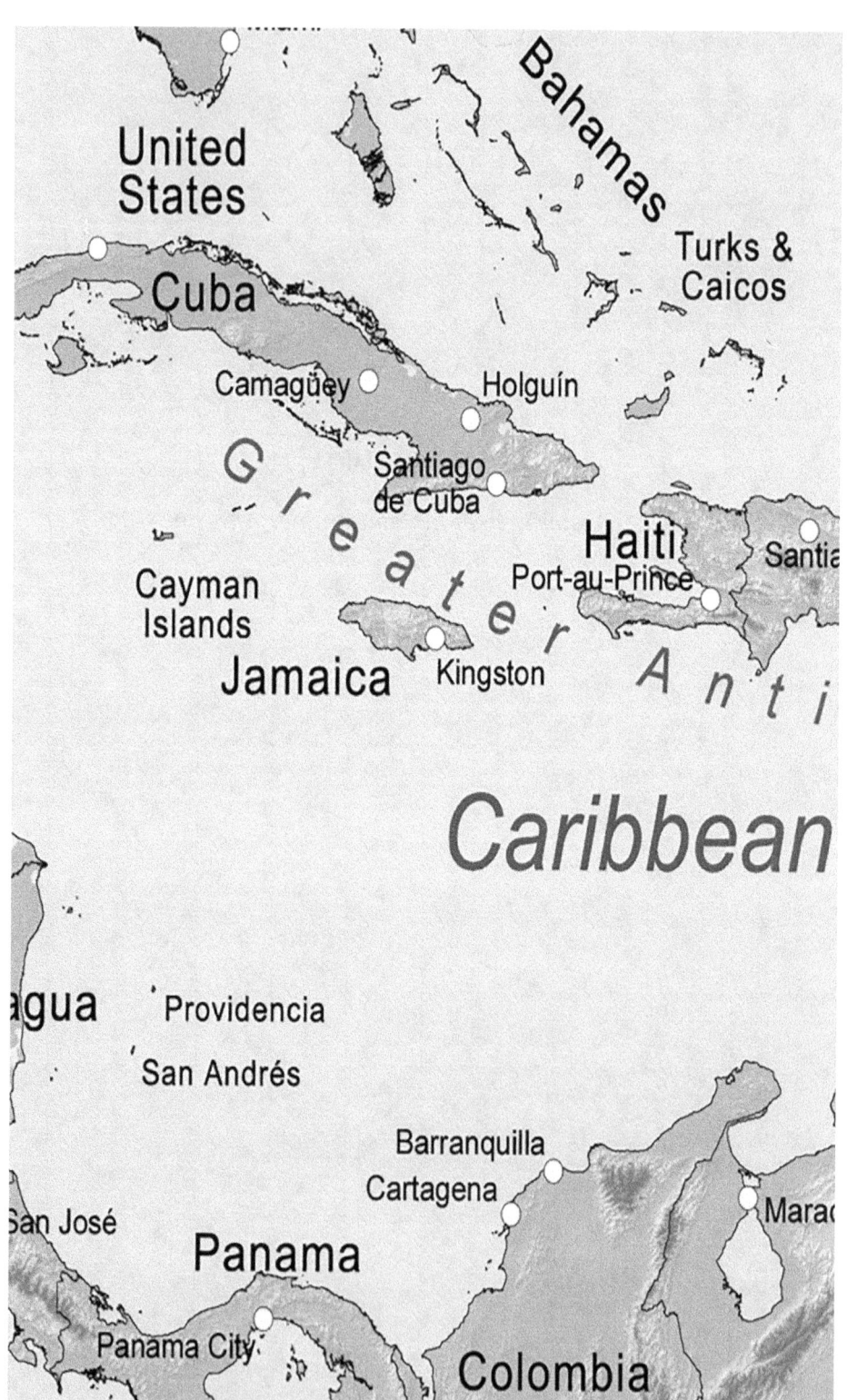

North
Atlantic
Ocean

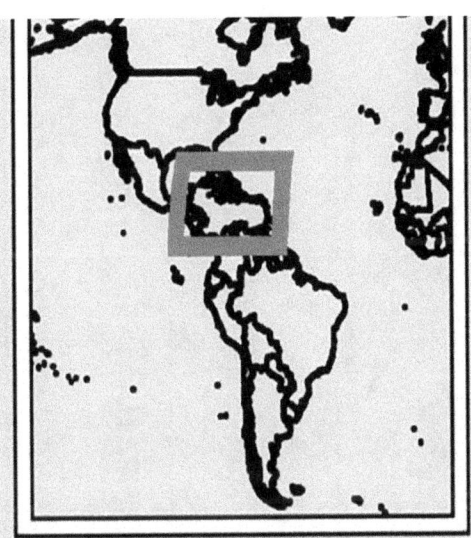

Dominican
Republic

Puerto
Rico

Virgin
Islands

Anguilla

St. Martin

Barbuda

ago

Santo
Domingo

San Juan

St. Kitts

Antigua

Nevis

Montserrat

I l e s

Guadeloupe

Sea

Dominica

Martinique

St. Lucia

Barbados

Aruba

Curaçao

Bonaire

Lesser Antilles

St.
Vincent

Leeward Antilles

Margarita

Windward Islands

Grenada

Tobago

caibo

Caracas

Barcelona

Trinidad

Venezuela

Leeward Islands

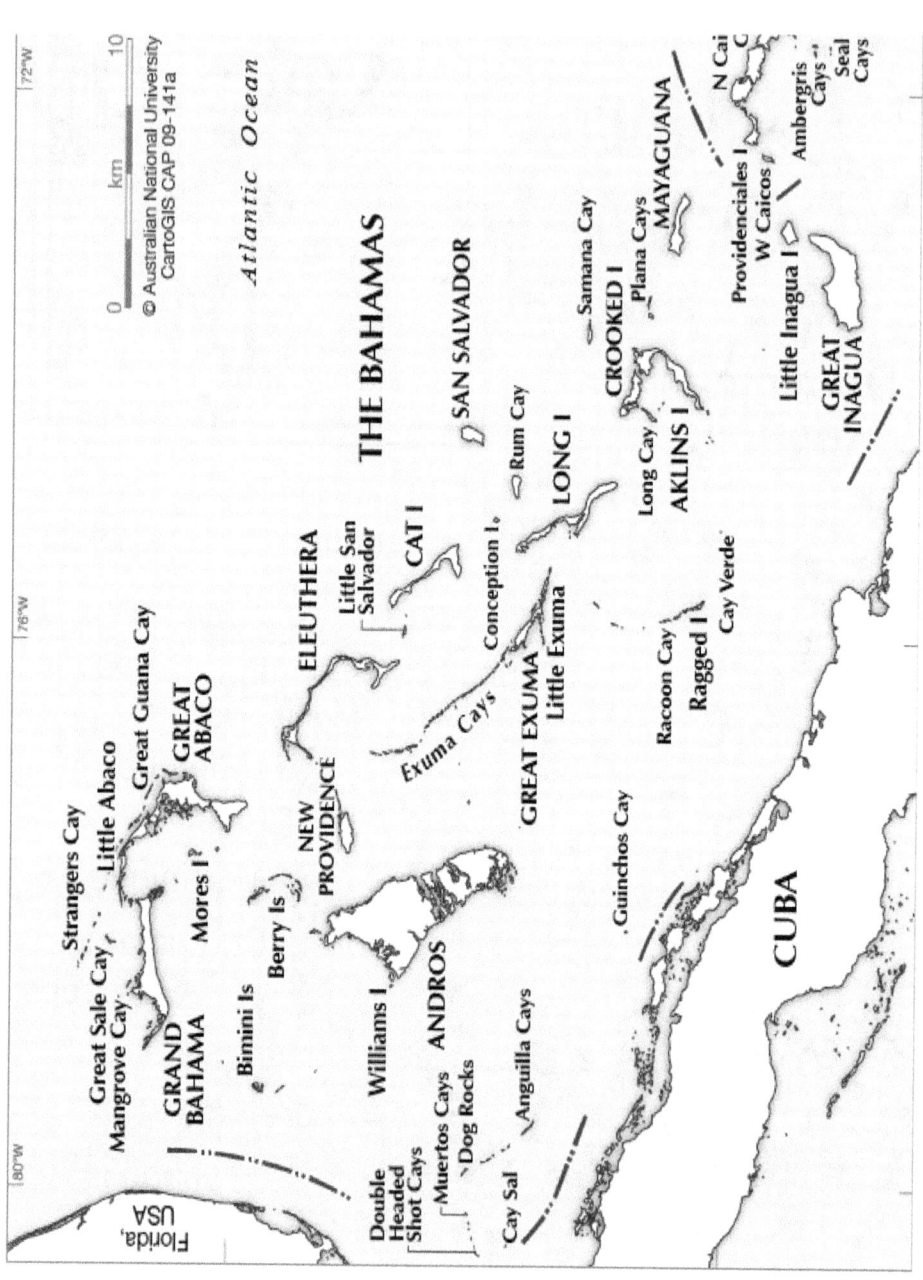

The Bahamas

PROLOGUE

COOPER CAIN WAS EXPECTING *a happy homecoming. It was later than expected by a few months, but that would only make it more special. But now...it was with the best news of all. Did they already know at home or was he the first to bring the news?*

The privateer, SeaFire, had just crossed the last sandbar with a good two feet of water beneath her keel. The prizes drew less water than SeaFire, so Cooper's mind moved on. He should have been home already. They would have been, but off the Cape Verde Islands a large convoy of Indiamen was sighted, along with an escort of several frigates and at least one two-decker.

SeaFire's crew was already doled out to their prizes, and not desiring a confrontation with the British frigates, Cooper had ordered the ships to sail toward Venezuela. There they were besieged by heavy squalls, leaving no option but to run southward. When the squalls were gone and the British convoy was now far away they came about. They hugged the coast of Venezuela and then passed Honduras.

They stopped at Roatan and old friendships were renewed as water and needed stores were taken on. When they set sail, they did so sailing northerly and then northeasterly, passing through the Yucatan Channel and into the Gulf of Mexico. Passing the Florida Keys, they sailed north again off the coast of Florida. It was here the sloop was sighted, a Bermuda sloop that was now a British dispatch vessel.

Cooper would try to out sail it, if possible, but if not, he'd turn and fight to protect their prizes. He'd just made a signal to Virgil on one of the prizes and Johannes on the other to 'make more sail' when a "**boom**" was heard.

Damme, but who does he expect to hit at that distance, Cooper thought.

The lookout called down, "The sloop has a white flag flying, Cap'n."

Cooper Cain paused to think. British naval captains all had a bag of tricks they'd pull from against the enemy. But he'd never known one that would dishonor a flag of truce.

"Heave to," Cooper ordered. "Let's see what this ship has on her mind."

The sloop was pierced for ten guns and a few swivels. No match for SeaFire, but Cooper had warned the lookout to be vigilant. The sloop closed within hailing distance and lay 'hove to'.

"Greetings to you, Captain. I'm Thomas Barley of the sloop, Swallow. It's my pleasure to tell you, sir, that peace has been signed between our nations."

Cooper couldn't believe his ears. "That is good news," he responded. "When was it signed, Captain?" Cooper asked, thinking of the two prizes that he was sailing home.

"What they are calling the Treaty of Ghent was signed this past December 24th. My admiral was told that the official date for the end of the war is this past February 17th. "

I'm good with the prizes, Cooper thought. He then asked, "Who is your admiral, sir?"

"Vice Admiral Sir Gabriel Anthony."

Cooper couldn't help but smile. "Captain Barley, you have just made my day. Your admiral is my father-in-law."

"You, sir, have shortened my mission then. I was to sail to Savannah and pass the word, had I not met up with you."

"Consider your mission complete then, Captain. Please tell your admiral to expect to see his daughter within the month."

"I will, sir, I assure you that I will."

The meeting with the sloop, Swallow, and Captain Barley had been two days ago. They were now almost home. His separation from Maddy would be over. As they rounded up and the anchor was dropped, a horde of people was making its way down to the river.

"I wish that I'd have fired a cannon," Cooper said to Quang.

"They might have fired back," Quang replied.

Looking about, Cooper spotted John Will. He didn't see Eli, though. Cooper turned and saw Mr. Ryker. "Are you glad to be home?"

"Aye, Captain, but I believe there will be some who might wonder what they'll do now with the war over."

Cooper stopped, Mr. Ryker's comments hitting home...and hitting hard. Over half of the crew had started out as pirates. The move to privateer was little more than a change in semantics, a different word... pirate, privateer. One was legal and the other one was not. The third officer might be young, but Cooper had to believe he was on target.

"Mr. Ryker, once the prizes are turned over and the ship is made clean, it's liberty for all hands except a watch. I will meet with the crew Monday. Right now, I'm going to see my wife and spread the word. The war is over."

CHAPTER ONE

ELI TAYLOR DROVE UP in a carriage with Maddy and Debbie. People were all around, shouting and cheering the war is over, it's over.

Maddy didn't hear a word as she rushed to her man. After a long embrace and passionate kiss, they paused.

"I was wondering if you could breathe," Eli joked, getting a slap on his shoulder from Debbie for his comments. "Is it true?" he asked. "Is the war over?"

It dawned on Maddy what was being said. "Is it, Coop? Did you bring the word that the war is over?"

"I did," Cooper replied. "I was stopped by one of your father's sloops. He flew a flag of truce and said the treaty was signed Christmas Eve and the war officially came to an end in February."

"Those prizes," Eli asked.

Cooper smiled, "Perfectly legal. One was taken on December 12th, and the other one was previous to that. We'd have been home sooner, were we not dodging convoys with frigate escorts, perverse winds and squalls. We could have had more prizes, had I wanted to take a slaver or two. But the two ships that I brought back are fully loaded with good cargoes."

"We have enough ships," Eli said. "What we'll need now is cargoes, trade goods to fill our ships' holds. We've done well as privateersmen. From here on though, it will be honest shipping."

"Er...that's something we will need to discuss with our crew, Eli. Some of those men have been with you since the *Raven*. This will bring about a big change in their lives."

Eli knew exactly what his young friend was referring to. "I may have a word with a few of them this afternoon, Coop. Mr. Brett is away right now, so I will help John Will see to the ships' cargoes. Do you want to be taken home, Debbie, or do you have things in Savannah to keep you busy?"

"Coop and Maddy can drop me off," Debbie said.

Quang was seated on a box under the eave of the warehouse office. Cooper made a motion with his head and the big Chinaman came over. He gave a bow to Maddy, who kissed him on the cheek.

"Thank you for watching over my man, Quang."

"Missy know Quang keep a good eye," he said, flushed at having been kissed.

"Quang, you can come with us or spend time in Savannah and come later," Cooper said.

"Quang come now," he replied. He was somewhat of a loner. He'd been loyal to Cooper and had been his cox'n for three years now. He gave Cooper his money to deposit into the bank. Quang spent very little on trollops, and less on alcohol.

Quang and Banty were at opposite ends of how they spent their prize money. Cooper had overheard Banty telling the first mate, Virgil Culpepper, about how he'd spent his last prize money. "I spent most of it on whores and rum. The rest of it, I wasted."

It had been hard for Cooper not to laugh, and Virgil had. But to men like Banty, who'd been 'brethren of the sea' there was no tomorrow. They played a dangerous game where you had no plans for tomorrow. Under Eli Taylor, and then Cooper Cain, they'd won the game so far. They'd beat the odds, but they'd lived like there was no tomorrow. There would be a change now, with the war ending.

Cooper and Maddy went home with Quang driving, after dropping Debbie off at her house. When they pulled up in the yard, Maddy gave Cooper a quick kiss.

"Go speak to Dagan. He said this morning that he thought you'd be home today."

"How is Dagan?" Cooper asked.

Maddy smiled, "Same as always. Maybe a little more misery when it rains."

Cooper smiled…more misery. That was something Rosa would say. She was the cook, maid, and the force that kept the house running…she and her daughter, Priscilla. Priscilla mostly helped Dagan but came running when Rosa called.

Maddy entered the house through the kitchen. Rosa was humming away as she went about her chores. "Rosa, the captain is back…and smells."

Rosa smiled, "I bet that didn't keep you from giving that man some sugar."

Maddy had learned that giving sugar meant kissing. "No, and I'm going to give him some more after a bath."

Rosa took a deep breath and sighed. "I don't blame you girl. You sho' got one fine looking man. I'll heat up some water for the tub."

"Do you want me to call Brand?" Maddy asked.

"No, child. When Rosa can't carry a bucket of water will be the day to put me out of my misery."

Cooper had talked to Dagan and now he walked into the house through the same kitchen door. He gave a Rosa a hug. "What's for supper?"

"You old devil," Rosa said. "It better be Ms. Maddy. I will fix you something special tomorrow."

"Coop!"

"Yo' wife beckons, sailor man," Rosa said. Cooper smiled and went to the bedroom.

"I've been waiting," Maddy said as she came to Cooper. She had taken off her clothes and had on a simple robe. Tears trickled down her face. "I'm so glad this war is over and I have you home."

Cooper reached out and pulled her to him. He kissed her long and hard. Maddy took the collar of her robe and wiped her face. The familiar smell was there. Her man smelled of the ship and sea. His lips still even had a slightly salty taste when he'd kissed her earlier that day. *Would it ever be different? Would he always be one with the sea like so many in her family?* How lucky Josie was. She didn't have to share James with the sea.

Maddy said, "Your bath is ready, Sir Pirate."

Cooper removed his pistols from his waistband and unbuckled his sword belt, laying them on a chair. Maddy moved his hands down as he went for his buttons, and she took over.

She unbuttoned his shirt, pausing to kiss his chest and stomach, as she knelt down to unfasten his britches. Cooper sat on the side of the bed as Maddy pulled first one boot and then the other off, dropping them of the floor.

Rosa, in the next room, hearing the boots fall, smiled a knowing smile and placed her hand over her heart.

After removing Cooper's boots, Maddy tugged at his britches and then his drawers. Maddy stepped back, now that she had her man's clothes off.

"I see that you are excited to see your wife." Maddy said this looking at his maleness.

"I'm excited to see more," Cooper replied.

"Show me then, Sir Pirate, or must I do all the work?"

Cooper rose up off the bed and drew Maddy to him. He tugged at the tie holding the robe closed, letting it fall to the floor. Cooper couldn't help but stare at his wife. The robe opened just enough to show most but not all of her breasts.

"Damn, but you look inviting," Cooper whispered as he continued to look at his wife.

"Is looking all you are going to do, Sir Pirate?"

"Not by a damn long shot," he said and roughly pulled her to him, pressing his body to his wife. He kissed her lips, face, and her neck, and then pulled the robe off letting it fall to the floor.

"Your bath is ready," Maddy whispered.

"It can wait," he said as he sat back on the bed and pulled Maddy to him. "I can't."

"Take your wench then, Sir Pirate. She is ready."

CHAPTER TWO

THE WEEK WENT BY so fast it was just a fog in Cooper's memory. At noon, the day after he'd returned, James and Josie came by, and with them was little Gabriel Marcus Anthony II. They had named the little man after James and Maddy's father.

"Father will be so proud," Maddy said.

"I told the sloop *Swallow's* captain to tell your father that we'd likely see him in a month," Cooper volunteered. "He will likely be recalled to England, now that the war is over."

Maddy smiled, "Yes, let's plan to leave right away."

James agreed also, and if possible they'd leave in the next seven to ten days. Cooper and Eli had talked to the crew of *SeaFire*. Most of them agreed to hang around until future plans could be made.

McKemie, the carpenter, would sail back to New Orleans with Buck Jewell, captain of *Thunderbolt*. Banty and Skeeter said that they would probably be drunk for a month but would talk with Cap'n Eli before they adopted any firm plans. Quang and Josiah would stay at Cooper's house. Cooper had told Luke to build a house, one with two apartments but with a central kitchen, dining area and sitting room.

William House, the stranded marine, would go to Antigua with Cooper and report in. Turner and Ryker Hall were both going home. Virgil Culpepper, Diamond, and Spurlock would stay around Savannah and maybe sign on to one of the company's ships. Johannes would likely retire. He'd saved most of his money for years now.

❋❋❋

THE DAY HAD COME to set sail. They decided to sail in the larger of the two prizes that Coop had taken before the war ended. While not strictly legal, as the paperwork had not made its way through the courts yet, the ship was renamed the *Lady Faith*, after Maddy and James' mother. If an inquiry as to the ship's whereabouts came up, it was to be told that she was being evaluated to see how sea worthy she was. A quick note to Virgil and he signed on to be the captain. Diamond and Spurlock unexpectedly signed on as temporary first and second mates.

Ox showed up then, on the day they were leaving. He explained, "Goose wanted to sail as well, but he had to go get Banty out of jail. Goose said that it may take either Cooper or Captain Eli to get Banty out. He tore up a fancy house when a man tried to horn in on his trollop." Sadly, Ox continued, "The other fella got the wench after Banty was hauled off to jail. All Banty got was a busted noggin', a near empty purse, and no mutton."

Banty needed to get to sea to get away from this trouble. Since Josiah was helping Josie with little Gabe, Cooper, Dagan, and Quang found their way to the jail. Goose had gotten nowhere, as a fine still had to be paid. Cooper paid the fine. With Banty still more drunk than sober, Goose carried his mate to the ship. Quang went to the inn where Banty and Skeeter were staying to get Banty's clothes. Yet when Quang got back to the ship, he had Skeeter over one shoulder and two bags of clothes in his hand. "He drunk," was Quang's explanation.

Gussie, who was nanny for little Gabe, was being helped aboard the ship. She was a freed black woman who'd never set foot out of the county. She was now trying to control her fear of 'getting on a ship that's going out in the deep water.'

The last person to board was not a surprise but hadn't been expected either. Jessie smiled as John Will carried her trunk on board. "Room for one more?" he asked.

A smiling Virgil answered, "Always."

☀☀☀

THE TRIP TO ANTIGUA went well. Several British warships were sighted a day out of Antigua. Maddy looked at each ship, trying to see if she recognized anyone. Maddy and James' brother, Jake, would now be captain of his own ship. When they arrived at the anchorage, in Antigua, Cooper took a boat to Gabe's flagship.

He was given permission to come on board, but got no further than the entry port. It apparently did not sit well with the watch lieutenant; Cooper's arrival from a ship flying the American flag.

"Your business, sir?" the lieutenant asked, not concealing his rancor.

Cooper started to snarl back, telling him to call someone with authority, but he didn't. "I'm Vice Admiral Anthony's son-in-law," he said. "I have his children on board yonder ship. I would be most grateful if you would have him notified."

The lieutenant's demeanor changed quickly. "Ah...yes sir. I will get Captain Davy."

"I'm here, Lieutenant." The captain dismissed the lieutenant and shook Cooper's hand. "It's a pleasure, Coop."

"Thank you, Captain Davy."

"Sir Gabe is in St. Johns. Faith is at home, however. Would my barge be of any use taking Maddy ashore?"

"Aye, it would, but I also have James, his wife, and little Gabe," Cooper said.

Davy smiled, "Little Gabe. I can see Sir Gabe now. I will send my barge over and send a lieutenant ashore to arrange transportation." He said this loud enough for the lieutenant to hear, adding, "I'm sure that he has nothing better to do."

A knock on the door sent Faith rushing to it. The servant was at the market and had taken her girl with her. Faith, opening the door, found herself staring James in the face.

"Hello, Mother, we've come to visit," James said.

Faith grabbed her son and pulled him to her, tears of joy flowing down her face. When she broke her hug, James said, "Josie and your grandson is here and so is Maddy."

Maddy smiled and said, "We are all here, Mother, even Dagan."

Everyone came in and greetings were made and then rooms were assigned. They had all gotten refreshed when a carriage could be heard outside.

"Stay here everyone," Faith said. She went to the door with little Gabe still in her arms and opened it.

As Gabe walked up, he was surprised to see his wife holding a baby. "Who is that?" he asked as he gave Faith a kiss.

Faith replied stunning her husband, "This is your namesake. Meet your grandson, Gabriel Marcus Anthony."

Gabe took the baby and looked at him. He certainly had the Anthony's features. "James is here," he asked, more a comment than a question.

Faith nodded, "Maddy and Coop are here, also."

Gabe smiled, "So, Sir Pirate has returned, hoping that his bringing our children home will keep me from hanging him."

Faith looked at her husband. His smile told her that he was joking. As he entered the great room to greet everyone, Maddy noticed the lock of gray hair that her father once had was almost covered by more gray filling in. He also had wrinkles around his eyes. Age was showing itself.

Once the children were hugged, greeted, and kissed, Gabe turned to Dagan. "Hello, Uncle. I have missed you." He then hugged the man, who had never left his side during the first war with the Colonies.

The next morning, Maddy went with Cooper to visit his mother and Jean Paul. They could see that Jean Paul was in the side yard exercising when the carriage pulled up. He was not expecting anyone so it was a bit of a surprise. Few people drove out this far unexpectedly. He was even more surprised when he saw that it was Cooper, his stepson and most prized fencing pupil, stepping from the carriage.

Greetings were made and then they went inside the house with Jean Paul calling, "Ann, we have a visitor."

Cooper's mother, seeing her son, ran to him.

❋ ❋ ❋

THE VISIT LASTED A month with, at least, one dinner party a week. Maddy was happy but quite exhausted by the time they were set to return to Georgia. The entire Anthony family got together the last night, including Gil, Lady Deborah, and Bart.

Cooper had asked Maddy, "Why does your uncle's wife like to be addressed as Lady Deborah and not Lady Anthony?"

"I'm not sure," Maddy said. "Strangers do address her as Lady Anthony, but people who know her, especially the Naval officers have always called her Lady Deborah."

During the meal Jake, the youngest of the Anthony children, said that he'd been practicing with Jean Paul while in port, and that his lessons had been used on a couple of occasions. He had apparently been boarded a couple of times but was triumphant on both occasions. They were not in the same circle with Cooper Cain.

"Very few are," Jean Paul said. Ann smiled but didn't like the talk of combat where her son might have been killed.

Gabe stood up then, clinking on his wine glass to get everyone's attention. "I want you all to know what a blessing it has been having our family together. Your mother and I have enjoyed this past month greatly. I want to be able to do more relaxing and be able to visit like we desire. I have been in the Royal Navy now for forty-two years, and that's long enough. Today, I sent a letter to the Admiralty advising them that as soon as my replacement is sent, I will haul down my flag and retire."

Faith reached up and took her husband's hand. Gabe looked down at his wife and added, "I'm sure that your mother has longed for this day for years now."

Cooper stood up and raised his glass, "A toast to the admiral and his lady."

CHAPTER THREE

THE PEACE HAD BEEN in effect a year now. It had been the longest time that Cooper could remember being home and sleeping in a bed next to his wife, since they'd married. Buck Jewell had sent word that he and Mary Ester were getting married and invited Coop, Maddy, Eli, and Debbie to the wedding.

Virgil had not proposed to Jessie yet, but she'd given him an ultimatum...marry her or find another person to share his bed. He had admitted to Cooper that he loved her but was afraid to commit.

Maddy had been spiteful in her comments. "If he doesn't marry her, I'll have Quang hold him down while I cut off his wedding tackle. Let him sit to pee." She had a temper when she felt that a friend was being wronged.

Virgil had taken a company ship to Bermuda. When he returned it was to get married or move on. Jonah Lee, their good friend, was now married but Moses hadn't. Maddy felt that if Jonah had tied the knot, there was no reason for Virgil not to follow suit.

Cooper had told Virgil before he left, "Marriage has not hurt Eli, Jonah, or myself." It was then that Virgil admitted his fear. Could he live with only one woman? He'd find out soon or Maddy would know the reason.

Mail was now possible between Antigua and Georgia via merchant ships. Maddy got a letter from her mother saying that a replacement for her father had been named and, her father was now retired. She promised that they'd visit soon, probably later that summer.

Eli came over that afternoon in an agitated mood. A company ship was to have returned a week ago and had not returned yet. Other than the cargo, he was expecting a letter from lawyer Meeks in regards to the sale of the Hotel Provincial.

"Maybe we need to go to New Orleans," Cooper suggested. "You can check on business and we can attend Buck Jewell's wedding."

***

THE *BONNIE ROSE* WAS a ship well founded. Her captain had been at sea, man and boy, for thirty-seven years. He'd rarely spent more than a couple of weeks at a time in port in all those years. The *Bonnie Rose* was his own ship. He'd purchased her with money made and saved as a captain for the Honest Johns, as the Honourable East India Company was known. The company's rules were rigid but he had profited and now he owned the *Bonnie Rose*.

Captain Percy Dorset had no complaints. He had no wife. Few women wanted a man who lived as he did. There had been women over the years, but never any children…that he knew of, anyway. His sister's son, Percy Hatcher, was his namesake. He'd taken his nephew to sea with him for the last seven years. He'd taught the boy well, and now the man Percy was his first mate. In a couple of years, Captain Percy would turn the *Bonnie Rose* over to his nephew.

They were four days out of Bermuda heading to Savannah, Georgia with a cargo for the Savannah Import/Export Company. Since England's war with her American cousins was over, the Bonnie Rose had made several trips to Savannah. Each trip was turning a handsome profit. *Ah… it was the perfect way to ease into retirement*, Captain Percy Dorset thought.

The sun was dipping its head over the horizon and the stern lanterns had been lit when a lookout mentioned a ship amidships on the starboard side, bearing down on them. Had it been a year ago, it would have been cause for alarm. But had it been a year ago, he'd have been sailing with a convoy, with warships as escorts. Percy still felt uneasy. He had too many years at sea not to. Should he put out the stern lights and darken ship? Was it the years at war that caused the unrest? Was it prudence or just an old man's nerves?

Percy called to his nephew, "Extinguish the stern lights and darken the ship. Let's then lay the old girl on a new course. I have a strange feeling about that ship."

Percy, the mate, thought that his uncle was being old and foolish, but he was still the captain. For another year or so, anyway. Once the stern lanterns were out, the captain ordered the few four-pound popguns loaded and had the small arms chest brought on deck. The moon was only a sliver, an eighth moon, so it was dark.

The mystery ship had not been sighted since changing course an hour ago. *Maybe we've lost them*, Percy thought. He called to his nephew to go to his cabin and bring him his night glass. He'd feel better if the sea was empty, after scanning it through the night glass.

Percy, the mate, stumbled in his uncle's cabin and banged his shin on a chest. "Damme, what's that doing there," he cursed. Taking a striker, he lit a candle. He moved the chest and got the night glass. He was almost out the cabin door when he remembered the candle. He turned back and blew out the candle. Rushing on deck, his shin bone hurt. Damned, but his uncle must be getting old to leave a chest out so.

His uncle, taking the night glass, scanned the horizon all the way around the ship feeling much better. He cautioned the watch to be vigil and at midnight, he went to his cot.

BOOM...BOOM!! The captain sat straight up. He slid his feet in his boots and made his way on deck. It was just dawn but there was that damnable ship.

BOOM...another cannon fired and this time it hit the fore-mast. The upper half of the mast toppled, bringing riggings and stays with it. Another boom, and this time the aim was better. The wheel was hit, killing the helmsman and turning the wheel into a mass of flying splinters.

"Heave to," the captain shouted, trying to figure out how the ship had found them.

The ship came alongside and grapples sailed across. One of the hands made ready to repel the boarders but he was hacked down by a rogue. Captain Percy looked for his nephew and found him lying in a pool of blood. A large splinter from the wheel was protruding from his gut. The captain of the rogues walked over to the ship.

"You gave me quite a chase, Captain. Had you not shown that last light, I would have lost you."

"Last light?" Captain Percy asked.

"Aye," Captain Rogue replied. "It was like providence. The sea was black, and then a light. A beacon, like it was saying here we are. It went out then, but we had a fix on ye by then."

Percy, the mate, was in agony. He'd die soon, but not soon enough. He'd been careless and stupid. He would now die for it. He'd caused the ship to be taken and lives to be lost. *Hurry death*, he prayed. His dreams were lost. His uncle's trust betrayed. "Oh...," he cried out.

Captain Percy looked at his nephew. He knew he would die, and it would be an agonizing death, having been impaled in the gut as he was. He turned toward his nephew only to be stopped by two of the rogues.

The rogues' captain stopped him from trying to get to the stricken man. "A friend?" he asked.

"My nephew," Captain Percy replied.

The rogue pulled his pistol and walked over to the groaning Percy and shot him in the head. He turned to Captain Percy, "It was a kindness. I hope someone will do the same for me, should the situation arise."

"I will gladly reciprocate," Captain Percy said.

The rogue captain smiled, "I'm sure you will. Now to show that I'm not a heartless man, I will allow you a keg of water, your navigation instrument, a supply of ship's biscuits and a boat."

One of the crew of the *Bonnie Lass* looked over the side. The blood from the dead men that the pirates had tossed over the side had attracted the sharks already. Two pirates dragged the mate Percy's body over, and when it hit the water, it was immediately attacked. The predators were now in frenzy.

"Any man wishing to join the brethren of the sea, step over here. The rest of ye lower a boat and be gone with ye before I change my mind."

The crew was down to eight men and the captain. It would be a crowded boat. Would they survive? It would be a chance and that was all. The boat was lowered and the men climbed down into it.

The rogue captain handed Captain Percy a pistol and a small bag, as he made to go down into the boat. "Powder and shot, if the going is too much to bear."

One of the rogues shouted and pointed, as the crew pulled away from the ship, "The coast is two days in that direction." He laughed and shouted again, "Hell is in the opposite direction."

CHAPTER FOUR

"DECK THAR, SOMETHING IS in the water off the larboard bow. Looks like a ship's boat."

Virgil Culpepper, the ship's master of the Savannah Imports/ Exports ship, *the Sassy Maid*, was headed home from Bermuda. Most of the ship's crew were former privateers and before that pirates. They had made the change to merchant seamen, albeit a tad reluctantly. The promise of good wages and freedom compared to a hangman's noose was the persuasion that finally won out.

Virgil had been in a daydream of sorts. When they returned to Savannah, he had to either marry Jessie or up anchor and sail for parts unknown. He loved the girl and she loved him. But his mother and father had loved each other once, and then they didn't. He could not remember hearing his mother ever once saying, 'I love you,' to his father. That had scarred him. He'd never been told what had happened between the two of them and he'd been too scared to ask. They'd both lived an existence, not a life. His sister had married and was happy, and then she'd died in childbirth. That had scarred him also.

Jessie and he slept together, and they had sex regularly. She was a most passionate woman. She could invent ways to satisfy him while making herself all the more desirable. Sometimes they made love, yet other times it was pure animalistic, provocative sex.

Jessie would often smile after they had tried something new and say, "Let's do that again, only this time..." If she couldn't satisfy a man he was either a sodomite or dead. Virgil wasn't too sure that she couldn't revive a dead man if he hadn't been dead long.

The lookout's cry of the boat in the water had interrupted his daydreaming. As he moved, he realized, not a moment too soon, that thinking of Jessie was having an effect on his manhood.

The boat was brought alongside the *Sassy Maid*. There were nine people in the small boat, sunburned and thirsty. They were brought on board and cared for. Surprisingly, the old captain, though sunburned with blisters on his face and cracked, oozing lips was in better shape than most of his seamen. He was given water and was soon able to speak.

He said, "Have a care, Captain. There are pirates about." He went on to explain how they were attacked by the pirates and his ship was taken.

Banty asked the captain to describe the pirate captain. After listening to the captain's description, he looked at Rooster and said, "That sounds like Frenchie LaFleur, doesn't it?"

"You know the scoundrel?" Old Captain Percy Dorset asked, rising up.

Virgil Culpepper placed his hand on Dorset's shoulder to calm the man. "He was a privateer when we knew him." Saying this, he gave Banty and Rooster a hard look.

"The sod has gone rogue now," Dorset swore.

Two days later, the *Sassy Maid* made her way up the Savannah River to the port. Virgil left Diamond in charge and took Captain Dorset up to the office. It was still early enough that Eli Taylor was there. Virgil introduced the two captains and explained what had taken place.

After talking with the captain, Eli reassured the man that they'd do everything in their power to see him back home. Eli then sent a rider to get Cooper and the Lees: Colonel Lee and Jonah. He wanted Moses, as well, if he was around. Moses had been spending time with an Indian girl in Florida.

❋❋❋

COOPER CAIN HAD SPENT the afternoon with Dagan, Maddy's uncle, and Luke, the overseer. It had rained a lot lately, and water coming off the hill had eroded the soil and created a wash, causing the road to the house from the main road to be almost impassable.

There was an area of red soil over near the river. It was full of gravel and had been left unused, as the red gravel played hell on the plow. They planned to fill in the ruts and the wash with the gravel. If that didn't help, they'd try to terrace the hillside.

The messenger delivered the note. Cooper handed the note to Dagan after reading it. "Come with me, Uncle," Cooper invited.

"I'm sure that it will prove more exciting than fixing the erosion," Dagan said, but at the same time a little voice inside seem to speak to him. *Squalls…a warning.*

Cooper called Quang to get a wagon ready while he went in to tell Maddy that he'd be gone for a while.

"Trouble?" she asked, not liking her husband being summoned for an emergency meeting.

Cooper had lived a dangerous life and Lady Luck would not last forever. Especially now of all times, when she might be pregnant. She'd not mentioned it to Cooper yet. She wouldn't, not until she was sure. She was a week late already. Rosa had said that was not uncommon. When she had gone six weeks since her last monthly, that would be soon enough to say something.

Maddy wanted to give Cooper a son. He deserved a son and a happy family life. Something that he'd never had. *Oh Mother, how I wish you were here*, she thought.

***

THE MEETING WAS OVER and a bottle of bourbon was passed around for everyone to have a drink. British Captain Percy Dorset felt a stinging of pain as the amber liquid passed his lips. Smacking his tender lips, he deemed the American drink to be passable. "Right passable," he said, using the words that he'd heard Eli Taylor use earlier.

As Dagan and Cooper climbed into the wagon, Quang, who'd stood in the shadows during the meeting, agreed with what Banty and Rooster had said. The captain of the pirates sounded like Frenchie LaFleur. Quang, though, didn't think the man had the financial ability to see the ship provisioned and organized. He could obtain a crew sure enough, but it had been Jean LaFitte who had been the brains and had the money. *So who had taken LaFitte's place now?*

When they got home, Quang told Cooper and Dagan his thoughts in his broken English. Cooper agreed once he thought about it. The ships under the Savannah Import/Export Company were all armed. The decision had been to increase the readiness of each ship. They would also be suspicious of any ship, regardless of friend or foe. However, there were no means to implement these rules immediately. Some of the company's ships were not due to return for six months. How many may already be lost without their knowledge? That was the hard part…the not knowing.

Maddy was still up when Cooper made it to the bedroom. After a kiss, Maddy asked, "Was the meeting at the tavern?"

Cooper smiled. "We had thought about it, but with so many of the local maidens yearning for my body we felt it best to hold it in the company office."

Maddy smiled, "You tell them, Sir Pirate, your wench be the jealous type. I'll cut off their catheads if they mess with you."

"Such talk from an admiral's daughter, no less. Where did you hear the term 'catheads'? Do you even know what they are?"

Maddy pulled her breasts from her nightgown and made most unladylike motions with them. *Damned if they weren't sore. Was that a change if you were pregnant?* She'd ask Rosa.

"Me thinks these be catheads, Sir Pirate?" she said.

"You think right," Cooper replied, leaning over and kissing one nipple and then the next. Maddy groaned and pulled his mouth back to her breast.

When Cooper was let go, he started to undress. "I've a question for you and a bit of spicy news."

Maddy helped Cooper out of his shirt and undid his britches. Cooper then sat down to take off his boots. "Virgil was at the meeting and he has decided to ask Jessie to marry him."

"Really," Maddy said as she pulled her nightgown over her head. She laid down on her stomach then and said, "Kiss my neck and back, Coop."

He did as he was asked. Nuzzling her neck soon had Maddy feeling good. She spread her legs and said, "Take me, Coop." He was only too happy to comply.

"Wait," Maddy said and tucked a pillow under her. "Now."

After they made love, Maddy whispered, "You like that?"

"Mumm," Cooper replied.

"That was how Jessie made love to Virgil before he left. It must have worked."

"Is that all you wenches do? Discuss how to beguile some helpless sailor?"

"We do compare notes," she said, raising her bottom up a bit to tantalize her man. "What was your question?" she asked.

"Would you like to go to New Orleans for a wedding?" Cooper replied.

"Yes," she said, wiggling her bottom again. "I believe that you might like an encore, Sir Pirate," feeling his manhood swell.

Cooper kissed his wife and whispered, "See what you do to me." He'd never tell her that Sophia had used the same position and other more exotic ones to bring him erect two or three times a night, during their short time together.

Sophia had been trained, of course, in the art of sexual exoticism, starting at the age of twelve. With Maddy though, it was just pure love for her man, with a little hint from Josie and Jessie along the way. He remembered Josie and Jessie flipping through the penny novels from Covent Garden when they were teens. Apparently, some of the stuff they'd read had come in useful... well, maybe not. If a woman had her mind set on a man, she'd usually get him, and very few had ever heard of London or Covent Garden.

CHAPTER FIVE

NEW ORLEANS, HOTEL PROVINCIAL... THE city, like the hotel was far different than anything Maddy was used to. Cooper sat in the carriage that had been hired at the waterfront. Debbie was with Cooper and Maddy.

Eli had spied two of the company ships in port, and had sent a signal to both ships using a code that he had developed for the ships. He had thought about using the Navy tradition of having each ship's captain to 'repair on board,' but had decided against it, thinking that it might seem high-handed. He signaled instead that he'd be coming on board. He intended to let them know the news of the pirates. They also needed to exercise their men at the guns. A good defense might well save the ship and their lives. As he rowed to the *Lady Grace,* fond memories of New Orleans came to mind. He wondered if Coop and Debbie were thinking about those past times as well.

Banty nudged him, "We be at the entry port, Captain."

⁕ ⁕ ⁕

COOPER HAD INSTRUCTED THE driver of the carriage to take the scenic tour of New Orleans on the way to the hotel.

Coop said to Maddy, "Bourbon Street has been described as the most decadent street in America." He pointed out the Bourbon Orleans Hotel when they'd driven down Orleans Street. "That's where the quadroon balls were held when I was last here."

Maddy had pointed out the very exotic looking Octoroon or quadroon women. Debbie had been quick to step in and explain how 'women of color' came to be quadroons and so on.

"What is a quadroon ball?" Maddy asked innocently.

Debbie looked at Cooper who pointed back at her to explain. She looked at Maddy and said, "The quadroon ball is where men of means went to purchase a mistress for themselves or for a son. These men would then purchase houses and give an allowance to these women in exchange for sexual favors. Sex would be for that man only. The women were mistresses and not prostitutes. Most of the men's wives accepted it without thought. Some actually liked not being bothered. Any children would be claimed and given the man's name and educated."

"All that just for sex?" Maddy asked, thinking how incredible it sounded.

"You have to understand that these women have been trained in the art of eroticism," Debbie said. "They know how to do things that most prostitutes never dreamed of." Maddy was still mulling this over when they arrived at the hotel.

The hotel was tucked under a stand of huge old oak trees. Walking into the entrance, Maddy couldn't get over the charm… the romantic charm. *Humm…did she think that because her mind had been on those women who were so exotic?*

A gentle breeze caused a chandelier to sway and reach the burning candles inside the globe. The flicker created vast shadows on the wall. She found herself gripping Cooper's hand. Jalousie windows lined the wall, much like those in the islands; only here under the oaks there was more of a breeze.

They hadn't gotten very far when a woman's squeal broke the silence. "Mz. Debbie." The woman, dressed to perfection, came from behind a small desk and rushed to Debbie. After the two greeted each other warmly, Debbie introduced Maddy.

"This is Madamoiselle Renee." After the two women shook hands as they do, Debbie then said, "I believe you remember Cooper."

Renee gave a wink and put on a big smile. "Indeed I do." She turned to Maddy and said, "Darling, you will be the absolute envy of every woman in New Orleans." She pronounced it as one word, "Nawleans."

Over the next several days, Cooper took Maddy around the city. Eli and Debbie came along sometimes. They had dinner with Lawyer Meeks and his wife, Carolyn. She filled Maddy in on how Coop and she had skinned some would be card players.

Caroline then whispered, "You may not know it but you will be the envy of most of the women in this town." She then smiled, "As beautiful as you are, it's easy to see how you won Coop over. You know there's a glow about you." Carolyn paused for a few seconds and then said, "You're pregnant, aren't you?"

"I'm not sure," Maddy replied.

Carolyn put her arm around Maddy. "Take it from an old woman, honey. You're pregnant." Maddy gave a sigh and smiled. "Does Coop know, Maddy?"

"Not yet, I wanted to wait until I was sure," Maddy replied.

Coop took Maddy to Pierre LaFitte's blacksmith shop the next day. "This is where I met Quang," Coop said.

Turning to the big Chinaman, Coop asked, "Do you remember it, Quang?" Quang nodded his head in reply to the question.

Pierre spotted them and wiped his hands on a dirty apron, and then hugged each one of them.

"Where's Jean these days?" Cooper asked. The question would have gotten a lot of men killed, but Jean and Cooper were friends.

"He's in Texas. He has a nice little setup in Galveston."

"The commodore should have been shot," Coop said.

"Yes, but he wasn't," Pierre replied.

While Jean LaFitte had been helping General Jackson, the commodore had raided and destroyed LaFitte's stronghold on Grand Terre.

"Jackson was beside himself, but what was done was done," Pierre said.

Eli and Debbie concluded their business by noon that day. The missing company ship had set sail on schedule but had not been heard from since. *Was it pirates, a storm or what?* Meeks had copies of all of Eli's transactions, so that was not lost. But the question of what happened to the ship remained. Would they find the answer?

Maddy snuggled close to Cooper in bed that night. "How much longer will we be here?"

"Buck's wedding is Saturday. This is Thursday. I would think that we could leave on Monday. Are you ready to go home?"

"Yes…Coop, I want to go see mother while I can travel."

"While you can travel," Coop replied.

"Yes," Maddy answered.

"Why wouldn't you be able to travel?" Coop inquired.

"Because I'm going to have your child," Maddy said.

"You are what!" Coop exclaimed.

"I'm going to have your child. You do want to have a child, don't you, Coop?"

"Yes," he said, pulling her to him and kissing her passionately.

Once the kiss was over, she laid on his chest looking at him. "Do you miss this…this life, Coop?"

"No…I'm not sure that I ever really enjoyed it," Coop replied.

"Not even the sex?"

Coop rose up, "I only had sex with Sophia. She was the only woman who moved me in this entire city, until you came along." He fluffed up two pillows and began to speak. "Sophia was much like the women Debbie told you about. She was only one-sixteenth black. I fell in love with her the first time I saw her. She was the mistress of a rich man's son. He got married so his brother tried to force himself upon her. The two brothers fought, and the elder son who was just married was killed. I bought Sophia from Henri d'Arcy for ten thousand dollars. I gave her papers to her, freeing her from her bondage. We were then married. We moved to Savannah with Eli, thinking we'd be away from the past and d'Arcy. It didn't turn out that way, though. I was away at sea and d'Arcy found Sophia. She fought him and in doing so, she fell, hitting her head on the balcony railing. It killed her instantly. Eli confronted the man, but before he could react, d'Arcy pulled a pistol and put a ball in his own brain."

Tears flowed from Maddy's eyes. She'd been told Sophia had died in a fall, but never the entire story.

Cooper pulled Maddy closer to him. "I always felt God had you in mind when he took Sophia…and then I realized that God didn't take Sophia, d'Arcy did. But you were still my gift from God."

Maddy whispered softly, "Make love to me, Coop."

"It won't hurt you?" Coop asked.

"No, silly," Maddy replied. "It's my first child, but even I know that."

After they made love, Maddy said, "Thank you, Coop, for telling me the whole story."

"I felt that you should know."

As they cuddled, Maddy wondered if she pleased Coop as well as Sophia had. She recalled Debbie's words then, 'You've made Coop happier than in any of the times since I have known him.' He was happy and that's what mattered.

CHAPTER SIX

BUCK JEWELL MARRIED MARY Esther in a small wedding. Mary Esther had asked for the wedding to be small but there were still one hundred people there. Buck asked Cooper, much to his surprise, to be his best man.

The wedding was held under some oak trees where a new church was being built. The fenced square provided the perfect area. Eli had commented that they'd broke ground for the new church in 1789. Hopefully, it would be finished before the carpenters needed burying.

Buck's wife, Mary Esther, and Maddy quickly became friends. With Debbie in tow, the three women enjoyed time spent shopping, and showing Maddy 'Naworleans'. Cooper and Eli informed Buck, who was the master of a company ship, about the threat of pirates. The main deck of Buck's ship, the *Crescent City*, could hold eight guns per side.

"Have her armed," Eli said. Cooper then added, "And a couple of carronades wouldn't hurt." Buck promised to put the orders in.

Eli, Debbie, Maddy, and Cooper went on board a steamboat that Sunday. Once on board, Eli leaned over and whispered, "We now own fifty-one percent of the company that runs this boat. We will send cargo down the Mississippi River to New Orleans, load it on ships and sail it to Europe, and maybe even the Orient."

Coop smiled. When Eli dreamed, he dreamed big. But in this case, Cooper felt it was more than a dream, especially if they could hold their own against the pirates. He felt a chill then. Nobody was ever able to hold their own against him. It was a sobering thought.

On the way from the steamboat they stopped and treated Maddy to a muffaletta. After the evening meal, Cooper took Maddy to a café by the river where he treated his wife to beignets and Café au lait. Cooper explained that Café au lait was chicory and coffee. Quang ate ten beignets and said, "Quang's favorite food."

The group set sail the next morning on board the *Lady Anne*. She was one of the ships in port the day they arrived. The other ship was being pierced to hold ten guns and the carronades as Cooper had suggested. A twenty-four pound smasher would hold its own with most anything the pirates would throw at them and would take fewer men to work it.

✳ ✳ ✳

WHEN SEAFIRE RETURNED FROM her voyage she was again fitted out as she'd been during the war. A sign was placed down at the company warehouse seeking *SeaFire's* old crew. Cooper even asked Virgil if he'd like to be the ship's captain.

"No, but I'll be your first officer," Virgil replied.

"You'll get masters pay," Cooper promised.

When the majority of the crew was together, Cooper explained that they would be escorting three company ships, first to Antigua, then to Havana, and lastly to San Juan. They were told of the pirates and that at that point at least one company ship had disappeared.

"We've no doubt Frenchie LaFleur was the one who took old Cap'n Dorset's ship," Banty swore.

"Aye," a couple chimed in.

Cooper asked, "Does anyone know where Spurlock might be?"

"I heard that he went to Charlestown," Skeeter said.

"Aye," Ox agreed. "Do you want us to go get him?"

"Yes, but only if you can go and be back in two weeks," Cooper replied.

"We'll be back," Ox said.

If only we had Johannes, Cooper thought. Johannes was now master on a company ship. A ship that was now due back...past due. *Was he now a victim, as well?*

❋ ❋ ❋

JESSIE AND VIRGIL WERE married near the banks overlooking the Wilmington River. After the reception, they spent their honeymoon weekend at the Washington Hall Hotel. The honeymoon would only last the weekend, as *SeaFire* had to be made ready for sea. That didn't mean, however, that the newlyweds would be parted, as Maddy had asked Jessie to come along. James and his wife were coming as well.

Eli had said, "It means the crew's quarters will be crowded, but they won't mind knowing the wages that they'll receive."

They had already discussed and decided against putting James, Josie, and little Gabriel, or little Gabe as he was called, on board one of the other ships. Dagan intended to come along as well, but he had volunteered to stand watch and sleep with the crew.

Ox and Skeeter returned the day after the wedding. Spurlock was with them, as was halfway expected, but so was Jimmy Spurlin, the hog man. "We brought Spurlin along, figuring that anyone who could shoot out a hog's eye ought to be useful," Spurlock said adding, "We rode by Doctor Cannington's house, but he was away."

A doctor would come in handy if needed. Hopefully however, on this trip a doctor wouldn't be needed.

***

JOHANNES EWERS WATCHED AS the unknown ship sailed parallel to them. He didn't like it. He'd received word from a British naval captain a few days ago that pirates were now plying these waters. *Was yonder ship a pirate?* It acted like one, and he, who had sailed under both the black flag and a Letter of Marque, knew when a ship acted as a predator and when they didn't. He had studied the ship in his telescope. She was being poorly handled. It didn't seem like a merchant ship. The evolutions on a merchantman might be slow, but they were done as befitting experienced sailors.

Johannes had not grown lax in gun drill, unlike some captains. The men on board his ship knew him as a firm but fair man who believed in drills. Sail handling, fire drill, and not the least of which was gun drill.

Johannes called his crew together. "I'm of a belief that yonder ship intends to do us harm. I don't intend to allow it. After dusk, I want every gun loaded and extra balls put close by. I know that we have a supply of grape. I want a measure on top of ball. We have three swivel guns and I want them loaded with grape and made ready. It will be uncomfortable but tonight we sleep on deck between the guns."

"Do we load both sides, Cap'n?"

"Aye, Mr. Sparks, that we do." Ewers added after a pause, "I'll be on deck as well. I think that I'll still fit into a hammock." This made the men laugh, as it was meant to do. "Mr. Sparks, if you will see that the men get an extra tot. Once it gets dark I want the ship darkened."

"We may not have time," a man named Stuart said. "That ship is closing."

Ewers didn't look at the ship. "Send the men to their stations, Mr. Sparks, quietly now." He then allowed himself to look at the closing ship. It was well armed. He could count twelve ports on the one side of the ship. Four more per side than what the *Ava* had. But while he knew their intentions, they didn't know his.

A single gun port on the pirate ship opened followed by several more. The sod had shown his hand far too quickly. It, at least, removed any questions as to her intentions.

Brown, the second mate, was acting as the gunner. He was not Spurlock, but he wasn't bad either.

"Mr. Brown!"

"Aye, Cap'n."

"I don't want the swivels fired until the pirate is alongside and ready to board us. The rogues will be bunched up then and we will get better results. Also, they've opened their starboard ports. I'm thinking that's a ploy, a plan to make us ready with one side but he plans to attack on the other. He may even try to cross our stern. I shall try to prevent that but be ready for either side. You may want to open our larboard ports as if we've taken the bait, but Mr. Brown, don't run out the guns until I say when to do it."

"Aye, Captain."

Johannes Ewers had played this game for many years now. He'd seen it played out enough to know the pirate captain might be dumb, or dumb like a fox, and that by playing to his actions he was actually setting you up for the kill.

BOOM!!! They had been fired on.

"Mr. Butterworth, make a log entry, fired on by possible pirate."

Butterworth was only twenty years old, and was the third mate on the ship. He had a lot of promise if he lived long enough.

The pirate's ship fired another cannon. The boom echoed across the water and the ball punched a hole in the fore topsail. The crew looked at Johannes. He ignored the opening shots. It would be dusk in another half hour. The rogue would want the attack over by then.

The pirate ship clamped on more sail and seemed to pull ahead. The sod would have done better to reduce sail and try to cross *Ava's* stern. Maybe he still would after running down their starboard side. *Damn, I wish that we had a bow chaser*, Johannes thought.

"He'll forge ahead and come about, Mr. Brown, so be ready," Johannes said.

"Aye, Cap'n," Brown responded, trying to keep the nervousness out of his voice.

The light in the sky was fading fast when the pirate ship came about and seemed to be approaching head on.

"She'll go starboard…I hope," Johannes said.

The men watched until they thought the pirate ship was going to collide, and then it started to pass down the starboard side.

"Open the gun ports, Mr. Brown. Fire as she bears. Make every shot count, men."

BOOM…BOOM…BOOM!!!

"The buggers firing chain shot to tear down our riggings and cripple us," Johannes said.

The first shots were too high but one of the next salvos found *Ava's* forward mast and hit about halfway up. Part of the shot thudded into the timber while the other part broke and cut into some stays.

Brown had *Ava's* guns firing now. She shuddered as her guns thundered forth. Orange flames of death lit up the fading sky. Brown had the men sponging out and reloading as soon as a gun fired. The speed was not up to *SeaFire* or *Raven's* standards, but for a merchant ship it was good.

Johannes ordered the helmsman, as the pirates sailed past, "Put your helm down. I'll not have her cross our stern."

Sparks walked over, "They know that we got teeth, Captain Ewers."

"Aye, they'll likely be more cautious when they pass again."

"You think they'll try again, Captain?" Sparks asked.

"Aye, Mr. Sparks, we'll feel her metal the next time. They just tried to cripple us that first pass."

"She's come about, Captain."

"Thank you, Mr. Butterworth. Tell me when she's near. Mr. Sparks, I intend to come about and meet her again."

Johannes spoke to the helmsman. "As soon as that ship passes I want to cross her stern. Be ready for my command." He then called up to the swivels. "If we pass close enough fire down at the quarterdeck and then reload."

The gunner threw up his arm indicating that he had heard and understood the captain's orders.

Johannes called to his crew then, "If you are not firing a gun, get down flat on the deck as the whoreson passes."

Ava had come about and once again the two ships were bearing down on each other.

"Mr. Brown, I think that he'll go to larboard this time."

"Aye, Captain."

The pirate ship fired first again, and like Johannes had predicted, she fired into the hull. The first ball slammed into the bow, sending the rail and crews head into the sky, nothing but splinters.

"He didn't have to hit the shitter," one man cursed, getting laughs from his mates.

Balls slammed in *Ava*, again and again, with Johannes feeling the ship shudder and groan as each ball slammed into her hull.

"She was not made for this," Sparks whined.

Ava fired back showing that she was not done for yet and twice ball and grape spewed into the pirate's gun ports overturning cannons and killing men. A bright flash let them know a charge of powder had been hit. Midway in the din of cannon fire, Johannes heard the bangs as the swivels were fired.

As they sailed past, Johannes ordered, "Now!" to the helmsman.

The ship canted and Butterworth slid down to the scuppers, as the ship swung around.

"Aim for the rudder, Mr. Brown. Every gun aim for the rudder," Johannes ordered.

No sooner had the ship returned to her normal sailing plane, than Brown had the guns firing. The pirate ship was fairly high up in the water, giving the gunners a better target. It was the fourth gunner who hit the rudder, smashing it. The next four blasted it until the entire rudder irons were torn loose from the stern post.

"She's crippled now, cease firing," Johannes said.

The night was upon them now, and Johannes said, "Mr. Sparks, go inspect the ship. Do not show a lantern where it might be seen."

After sailing west for an hour, Johannes brought the ship back on course and sailed toward Savannah. Mr. Sparks reported a few stove-in planks at the waterline but most of the damage was between wind and water.

"When it gets light enough to see, check the forward mast. I know that it took a hit. Mr. Butterworth, how are the men?"

"A few cuts and bruises, but nothing serious, Captain," Butterworth replied.

"Mr. Brown, you did well. If I didn't know better, I'd swear that you've had experience in action."

"Aye, Cap'n, I was the gun captain in the Royal Navy back in '82."

"It showed, and thank you," Johannes replied.

"The swivel guns cut down most of the rogues about the quarterdeck, Captain," Brown said.

"I'm sure that helped there at the end," Johannes said.

"I'm sure it did," Brown answered his captain.

"Now, about that ration I'd mentioned. Let's see that everyone gets a full cup," Johannes ordered.

It was two days later when they made it to Savannah.

CHAPTER SEVEN

W HEN *Ava* WAS SIGHTED, word was quickly sent to the office of Savannah Import and Export. By the time Johannes made his way to the office, Michael Brett had sent word to Eli and Cooper who were enjoying a noon time meal and a pint of beer.

"I'll never get used to this type of beer," Eli complained. He'd always enjoyed the dark stout beer still served in many taverns and establishments in New Orleans.

In Savannah, with the Revolution still in mind and fewer Europeans visiting, the local brewers made a lager that was clearer or lighter than the dark stouts Eli enjoyed.

When beer was mentioned once, Eli snarled, "If George Washington loved Porter, why shouldn't I."

Coop had drunk Porter in England. It had been popular there. Coop had pointed out to Eli once that Porter was not a stout beer. He got a glare for his comments. The Turks' owner pointed out that while old George probably had to drink the Porter on occasion, it was not what he made.

"He made small beer," Eli threw back. "Do I look like a child?"

Turks did serve a good meal, so Coop and Eli still frequented the place. When Eli was alone, though, the owner didn't come to the table, he stayed behind the bar.

When the boy came with the message, "Cap'n Ewers be back," Coop flipped him a coin while Eli paid for their meal. The two had walked to the tavern. Now, a cab was not around so they returned at a brisk pace. When they got to the office, both men were nearly out of breath. Surprisingly, Eli didn't seem to be as bad as Cooper. It was something Cooper swore to remedy. Soft living over the past year had robbed him of his wind…and his waist too, if he'd admit it. If he didn't, his britches would remind him every morning.

The two men quickly shook hands with Johannes and welcomed him back. A glass of Old Jake Beam Sour was passed around. A barrel had just been given to the company.

Eli smacked his lips, after a drink, and said, "Buy a hundred barrels. We'll make a fortune." One hundred wasn't available, but they did buy ten barrels.

Cooper had even taken a cask to Maddy's father.

Johannes gave a thorough narrative of the pirate's attack, while they sipped at their whiskey. "Mr. Brown, our acting gunner, says the main top swivel gunner swears that he cut down all the rogues on the quarterdeck on our last pass. He likely did as, when we crossed the ship's stern there was no attempt to evade us."

When Johannes finished his statement John Will stood up and shook Johannes' hand again. "The company and the crew were lucky to have such an experienced man in command." Eli and Cooper agreed with him. John Will continued, "After the cargo is unloaded, we need to see if Mr. Watts can give the ship a thorough inspection." Mr. Robert Watts had a shipyard at Yamacraw.

Johannes appeared tired so Michael Brett sent a runner to the Washington Hall Hotel to reserve a suite for Captain Johannes Ewers. "He is to have anything he wants including room, beverage, food, and…ere a companion if he wishes. Have the hotel send the bill to the company's office."

The glass clinked loudly as the top of the decanter holding the Beam's Whiskey was replaced. Everyone turned to Eli, whose hand still rested on the top of the decanter.

Eli looked at each of them and said, "We've got a new threat, gentlemen. Unlike the war that just passed, not only are our ships and cargoes in danger, but so are our people. Johannes Ewers is as good a man to command a ship as there is. Had he not demanded guns, powder, and shot, we'd be like old Captain Dorset, a lot poorer."

"We've agreed to properly arm our ships, Eli. What more can we do?"

Eli paused before he answered. He saw that his glass still had a bit of amber liquid in it, so he downed the remainder and set the glass back down. "It's time that we talk to our political friends, especially those who made money during our privateering days. We need to tell them to contact the Navy. It will give them something to do now that the war is over."

✻✻✻

THE FOLLOWING DAY COOPER went to the hotel just before noon. Johannes was dressed and about to go down to the ship. Cooper explained to Johannes that he wanted him to assume command of the *SeaFire* for the trip to Antigua and possibly until the pirate problem was dealt with. Johannes listened but didn't comment.

The two men grabbed a pint and had a plate of oysters before walking down to the dock. A pretty wench came over to their table and, putting her arm over Johannes' shoulder, asked if he needed anything…anything else at all.

"No," he said, a little flushed at the woman's open invitation in front of Cooper. When he took out his purse, she laid a hand on it.

She put the index finger on her other hand to her lips. Kissing it, she placed it on Johannes forehead. "It's all taken care of, dearie."

Coop couldn't help but smile as the girl slowly dragged her hand across Johannes shoulder and down his arm. "I believe that you have an invitation for dessert, my friend. Should I come back later?"

Johannes gave Coop a hard look and said, "Let's be on our way." He did flip a coin to the wench.

By the time they got to the *Ava*, Cooper had explained the plans to Johannes, including the passengers. Coop then promised that there'd be no reduction in pay.

"Do you think pay would make a difference, Coop?" Johannes asked.

"No, but you had to be told."

Johannes nodded but didn't speak. When he did he caught Cooper off guard. "So, it's a father you are going to be. When I first met you, I was not sure if you even knew what that thing was good for besides making water. You sure didn't know a thing about a ship, but the captain saw something in you. It was something we all came to see. You are a good man, Cooper Cain, and you'll make a good father. I'm proud to be your friend and I'd be proud to command the *SeaFire*. When do we weigh anchor?"

"Next Monday" Cooper replied.

Johannes nodded. "My chest will be ready."

Heading home, Cooper felt lighthearted. Most of his crew would be back with him. They were men that he knew and trusted, and also men who were not afraid of violence. Men like Ox, who'd kill a man as quick as you please if Coop ordered it, yet who would pick up a lady or a child and take them across a muddy street. He'd give his last coin to a person in need, but if a man cheated or wronged him, the odds were against that person seeing a new day without a sincere apology. Most of the crew was like that. Men born of the sea and, if the truth be known, they would rather die at sea. A hard lot…but they were his lot, his and Eli Taylor's.

❋❋❋

THE DAY TO SAIL finally arrived and so did Maddy's morning sickness. She was miserable for the first hour that she was up. Rosa helped her with the sickness. She'd mixed up a batch of ginger tea to drink. This really seemed to help Maddy. Rosa sent a bag full of roots to steep and make more tea when what she'd sent ran out. She also gave Maddy a small bottle of peppermint oil. When Maddy couldn't drink the tea, she could remove the bottle cap and sniff the peppermint and it would quickly ease her symptoms.

Coop had talked to Luke, his overseer, about seeing Eli if an emergency came up or there was a need for funds beyond what he'd left him. Luke smiled all the time that Coop was talking. It dawned on Cooper then that Luke had a better feel for taking care of the place than he did. He did the job all the time when Cooper was at sea without any help. Cooper had thought about bringing Rosa, but she'd said that she didn't like a pond much less a river. And the ocean, Lawd there was no way. Josiah would have to take up where Rosa had left off.

CHAPTER EIGHT

THE TRIP TO ANTIGUA went as smoothly as possible. They'd hit one small squall that lasted only a few hours as Johannes had predicted. They were on the third day at sea before another ship was sighted. It never closed so there was no identifying the ship.

Maddy pulled Cooper to her that night, "Oh damn, Coop."

"What Maddy?" Cooper asked her.

"What if mother and father are not there? What if they went to England or somewhere else?"

Coop kissed his wife, "What if has no bearing. If they're gone, we'll visit my mother and Jean Paul, our other friends, and if we have missed them, which I doubt, I'll go get them."

Turning toward Coop, Maddy had pushed her breast against his chest. He could feel himself getting excited, but there was only a makeshift screen that separated them from James and Josie. There'd be no making love until they got to Antigua. The thought made Cooper think, *please Lord don't let the wind fail us now.*

✱✱✱

IT TOOK TWO CARRIAGES and a wagon to take everyone to the Anthonys' house. Bart opened the door when Maddy knocked. "A first," Maddy said, "Bart is speechless."

Bart was Vice Admiral Lord Gilbert Anthony's cox'n. He'd been Uncle Bart when Maddy was growing up, just like Jacob Hex was Uncle Jake.

"Are Uncle Gil and Aunt Deborah here?" Maddy asked.

"Yes, I was just going to get the coachman to bring the carriage around. I 'spect he can wait a while longer now."

Maddy put her finger to her lips to 'shh' Bart as he started to call out. She kissed him on the cheek and then walked around him into the great room. Nobody noticed at first as they were all engaged in conversion.

Faith finally turned and saw her daughter. Tears of joy started flowing as she rushed to her daughter, "Oh, Maddy, you're home."

After greetings and introductions were made by everyone, and with Grandmother Faith holding little Gabe, Maddy cleared her throat.

"You are probably wondering why we all came to visit. Besides the fact, that we all wanted to see you, I wanted to be with my parents while I could. You see, Sir Pirate has me with child."

Everyone was silent for a moment and Coop was thinking, *you didn't have to say 'Sir Pirate,' you know your father hates that.*

Faith, still holding little Gabe, walked over and hugged her daughter. She then hugged and kissed Cooper. "You better take care of my daughter and grandchild, Sir Pirate," she whispered. Faith smiled then and squeezed his arm.

Gabe followed suit, only he said, "Congratulations."

Deborah and Gil were next in line, followed by Jake Hex. Gil called to Bart then, "Send someone down to the inn to prepare a feast for tonight."

The next morning they carried the news to Cooper's mother and Jean Paul. His mother, Ann, was also excited to see the twins. They had always been close, back in England.

Gabe and Cooper, later that day, stopped in to see Sir Robert Basnight, Governor of Antigua, and Cooper's old friend. They couldn't stay long as the governor had appointments. Their conversation, however, had touched briefly on the pirates. They'd been taking British ships, just as they were the American ships, so neither country seemed to be immune from the blackhearts.

A thought came to Sir Robert then. He wanted to pursue the conversation with Coop but at a more convenient time. *Who better to find out about pirates than a pirate? Yes, Cooper Cain had arrived at a most opportune time.*

❋❋❋

CAPTAIN DAVID DAVY DIDN'T know why he'd been summoned to the Admiralty. The war was over, and his ship was paid off and he'd expected to spend some time, perhaps the rest of his life, on the beach. Ariel and he had been the guests of Lord and Lady Stanhope the previous evening. Lady Stanhope was Gabe's, Vice Admiral Sir Gabriel Anthony's mother, Maria. She had married Lord Stanhope.

Ariel had lived with Maria for periods of time when Davy had been at sea, usually with Gabe. For the last six years, he'd been Gabe's flag captain. Those had been good years. Davy had never expected to rise to the lofty rank of captain. He'd been sent to sea by a squire who was more interested in his mother's ample bosom than he was looking out for young Davy's career. It had, at least, gotten him his billet as a midshipman. It was there that he met Gabe Anthony. Gabe was the senior mid and he was the junior. Their lives had been forever connected from that day on. It was Gabe who'd given him command of his first ship. It was also Gabe's uncle who had brought Ariel into his life. He couldn't count the times that he'd sailed into battle under Gabe's flag.

After the war, Gabe had retired; therefore, ending the reign of the Fighting Anthonys in the British Navy, at least for the time being. The title had started with Gabe's father, James, a vice admiral, and passed to his eldest son, Gil, a vice admiral, and then on to Gabe, who lowered his flag as a vice admiral. The chain had been broken there.

Faith and Gabe's oldest son chose the land, a farmer, taking after Faith's family. Maddy, their daughter, a girl who had stolen the hearts of every sailor in Gabe's fleet, had married a pirate, turned privateer in the last war. Would any son of theirs turn to the sea as his father and grandfather? Then there was Jake, Gabe's youngest son and now a captain. But with no war to fight, would he gain the Fighting Anthony title? Jake had been named after Gabe's cox'n. Jake Hex had saved Gabe's life, years ago, at a moment of carelessness by Gabe. Since then, they were forever together. Jake had made full captains tremble with just a glare. Next to Gabe, the legendary cox'n pulled more weight than anyone. A word from him and lieutenants jumped, captains nodded their heads, and women threw themselves upon him. He was Uncle Jake to the Anthony children. He was a man that you didn't trifle with to everyone else.

Davy had had good cox'ns but none that he'd felt the least bit endowed to.

✳✳✳

"Captain David Davy," Davy said, showing the official summons to the clerk. Without the summons, he'd have been just another captain seeking employment. He was probably towards the top of seniority on the captain's list by now. But the list meant little, he knew. Gabe and Gil had both been lucky to rise up the list as quick as they did. However, many captains chose to retire rather than fight their American cousins back in 1775 and 1776. Right time and right spot. If the Lords of the Admiralty wanted a senior captain for an assignment, he fit the billet.

Davy had just seated himself when the First Lord's secretary called to him. *Was this to be a plum assignment or would he be off chasing slavers with the slavery patrol? If that was it, would he turn it down*? He'd not subject Ariel to that climate or conditions. He had the means for them to live comfortably and better than most captains. No, if that was it, he'd turn it down and retire. With his mind made up, he followed the nasal sounding secretary into the First Lord's chamber.

***

VISCOUNT MELVILLE WAS LOOKING out his window with a clay pipe in his hand. Gray clouds hovered over the city making it damp in Melville's office. A small fire in the fireplace was losing its battle against the dampness. Davy thought that he could detect the slight odor of mold. The secretary announced Davy and then retreated.

Melville stood at the window a full thirty seconds after Davy was announced. It was long enough to make the moment tense. The First Lord turned and a frown left his face and a smile took over. *Something is bothering the man,* Davy thought. *Hopefully it's not me.*

Melville shook Davy's hand and beckoned him to a chair. "Would you care for tea?" Melville asked, ringing a bell.

A servant appeared with a tray carrying two cups of tea before Davy could decline. After inquiring how Davy took his tea, the servant withdrew. The tea did seem to help with the chill, Davy decided.

"I've been reading your records, Captain. Gabe has been most courteous in his praise of you and your abilities. He's even gone so far to say if an officer could be promoted on ability as opposed to seniority, you'd have raised your flag years ago."

Davy wasn't sure what to say, and then finally got out, "Sir Gabe is most kind, sir."

Melville continued, "It seems the rogues who raided our ships under the guise of privateers, during this recent unrest with our Colonies, have now dropped the disguise and are openly preying on our ships. So much so, that Governor Basnight has asked for a force to deal with these blackhearts." He paused and sipped his tea.

Davy had noticed that he still referred to the United States as Colonies. He also wondered if Melville knew Gabe's son-in-law had been a privateer...surely he did.

Melville continued, after taking a napkin and wiping his mouth, "Your record shows, and Sir Gabe has informed Governor Basnight, that you've had an abundance of experience dealing with rogues dating back to your days under Lord Anthony." Davy nodded, not thinking that an answer was desired. "Governor Basnight, along with an endorsement from Sir Gabe, has requested that you be assigned to the West Indies to scour the seas for these pirates. He also thinks 'who better to find a pirate than a pirate', meaning Sir Gabe's son-in-law. It is my understanding that he has done a great service to Sir Robert and is a man to be trusted."

"I would trust him with my life," Davy volunteered.

"You may have to, Admiral Davy. I concur with the request and recommendations of Sir Robert Basnight and Sir Gabe. You are to be assigned as Commander in Chief of the West Indies with the authority to use any measures necessary to rid the seas of these pirate rogues. That includes hiring Sir Gabe's pirate son-in-law." Davy was about to object to Melville's words when he saw the First Lord smile.

"Sir Robert feels and I agree that Cooper Cain should carry out his hunt independently, but will call on you for support. Your squadron will be made up of frigates, brigs, and one armed cutter. Sir Robert says that Cain feels any ship larger than a frigate would be useless."

"He would know," Davy said. "We never caught him."

"Two other things, Admiral, your flagship will be the *Minotaur* 74. She was built in 1793 and is just completing a refit in the shipyard at Portsmouth. She does not have a captain as of yet. I thought it best to let you pick your own flag captain. I do know that Jake Anthony's ship just paid off. He is young and has never commanded anything larger than a frigate. He is an Anthony, however, and has been bred for the sea. If you want him, I will have his orders drawn up immediately and you can personally take them to him. He is living at Gabe's mother's house at the present. If you wish for someone senior, I will give you a list of available captains. I will then give Jake another frigate to be assigned under your flag, as a favor to Sir Gabe."

"I will be glad to have Jake as my flag captain, sir." Davy had a moment to ponder his decision, and it was not lost on Melville.

"It's better to decide now, rather than see Captain Anthony fail and have to be replaced later," Melville said.

"Thank you, sir. You read my mind, but I will stick by my decision. I've never seen an Anthony fail yet," Davy replied.

Davy left Whitehall with a conflict of emotions. He'd made admiral, and that was something more than he'd have believed just yesterday. Ariel would be pleased. What bothered him was being told to support Cain. He did trust the man, but didn't like being told to give Cooper what he wanted. A damn pirate telling an admiral what to do, that was a blow to the normal routine, and he didn't like it.

CHAPTER NINE

GOVERNOR SIR ROBERT BASNIGHT sat at his desk in deep thought. He'd had a meal with all the Anthonys and Cooper Cain last evening and drank too much wine. If there was a man to unseat Sir Gabe in daring and fighting ability, it would be Cooper Cain. Of course, Jake, Sir Gabe's youngest son hadn't had the opportunities as his father. Cooper had made many of his own opportunities, albeit illegally. What troubled Sir Robert now, he had to admit, was what he was going to ask of Cooper Cain.

The Navy would send a force to seek out and destroy the pirates. Melville had sent a letter agreeing to that. Admiral Davy would be here within the month with a squadron of frigates and brigs of war. But who better to catch a pirate, than a pirate. Cooper Cain was that man, but his wife was pregnant. She'd need someone with her…Faith. A girl should have her mother with her when giving birth to her first child. Maddy would want to be in her home when the child was born. Would Faith travel to Georgia? Probably, since there was nothing on Antigua to keep them tied down.

Sir Robert felt another wave of dyspepsia. Was it the wine or what he was about to ask of Cooper when he got there? He rang for his servant and asked for a small glass of pickle juice. Hopefully it would help him.

Cooper arrived at ten o'clock and with him was Dagan, Sir Gabe's uncle, protector and advisor. Dagan was now Maddy's protector as well. At least he was from all the stories that Sir Robert had heard.

Two villains had once been sent to murder Maddy as a means of revenge, since Cooper had stripped his cousin of his wealth. Of course, that action had been revenge itself, for all the lies Cooper's cousin had told and for the ugly scar that Cooper still carried across his face. It was a scar that men would think offensive, but to women it seemed to be a magnet.

Tea was served, but Sir Robert's cup of tea seemed to have lost its flavor due to the pickle juice that he drank. He set it aside and came to the point.

Sir Robert, choosing his words carefully, began, "It seems that we've been beset upon by a band of pirates, Coop, and they are raiding both of our countries. I understand that your company has personally seen losses."

"Aye, we have and would have lost more, had not one of my... previous men not had the experience necessary to deal with the attack," Cooper replied.

Sir Robert knew what Coop meant by experienced hands. He'd met Johannes Ewers while on passage to Antigua some years ago. He was a likable man but no doubt a dangerous foe.

"Coop, I've sent for a squadron of ships to deal with the pirates, but commanders who have no experience in dealing with this scourge can do little more than patrol and investigate. They may get lucky on occasion but more often than not, they'll fail to bring the whoresons to battle. We need a man with...," Sir Robert paused, thinking of the right word. "A man who has insight and cunning, and understands that this is not a gentleman's game, and who is not afraid to take the necessary actions to rid these seas of the vermin that would harm our ships, our countries, and our very own women. That man is you, Coop. I'm prepared to give you all that you will need including the cooperation of the

Navy. Sir Gabe's old flag captain has been promoted to admiral and will be here soon with ships to help."

Cooper looked at Dagan. They didn't need to speak, each one of them with one person on their minds…Maddy! Cooper stood and said, "I will give you my answer within the week."

The men shook hands and Coop and Dagan left. As they were walking toward the carriage that waited for them outside Government House, Cooper spoke, "What will she say, Dagan?"

"I wish that I knew, Coop, but I do see you coming home before the baby is born," Dagan replied. This is not something that either wanted to bring up to Maddy.

Several horses were tied up outside the Anthonys' house. As Coop and Dagan walked inside, the first visitor that Coop saw was Buck Jewell.

"Buck, it's good to see you."

"Aye, and you as well, Coop. I just wish it was better circum-stances. We were a day from Antigua when we were set upon by the pirates. Two ships were working together. I could have defeated one but not both of them. We were given two boats and a keg of water for each."

"Damnation," Cooper said. "Who are these rogues?"

"I don't know, Coop, but one of my crew heard one of the pirates say that Calico would be happy with them taking a Savannah ship."

Cooper lay next to Maddy that night. He was gently rubbing her stomach. "My belly is growing," she said.

"Aye, but you look more beautiful than ever," Cooper replied.

"You lie, Cooper Cain."

"No, Maddy, I'd never lie to you."

"Hold me, Coop. Hold me close."

Cooper drew his wife to him. After a minute or so, he felt a tear fall on his chest. He raised up and took the sheet to wipe Maddy's eyes. "Why are you crying, my love?"

"You're leaving. You are going after the bastards attacking our ships," she said.

Cooper was taken aback. Maddy rarely cussed but when she did it was venomous. 'Takes after Faith,' Gabe had warned him. He'd never heard a woman cuss like Faith did at times, with Nanny scolding her at every turn.

"Not if you are against it," Cooper said,

"I'd be a fool to let them tear down what has taken years to achieve, Cooper. I have to think, we have to think, of our son."

"Our son?" Cooper asked.

"You doubt that you have a son on the way, Sir Pirate?"

"No, Maddy, I don't doubt anything you say."

She sat up then, "It won't take you long to…to destroy these devils, will it, Coop?"

"No, I couldn't stand being away from you too long, my love," he said.

"You will be back before your son is born then. I think that we shall name him Eli Anthony Cain, after his grandfathers."

"Eli is not his grandfather," Cooper replied.

"He might as well be. He treats you like a son. You never knew your father, and he never had a son, so you two fit."

"What about Dagan?"

"We'll do like the Spanish do. We'll add Dagan in there and he can have a slew of names," Maddy said. Coop smiled, 'slew' was a word that Rosa used.

The next morning, at breakfast, Maddy spoke, "Mother, would you and father like to come spend some time with me until the baby is born? Cooper is going to kill pirates."

A hush fell over the table. Nobody knew what to say to Maddy's blunt announcement.

"You can spend some time with James, as well. We've room, but I'm sure that Dagan will go with Coop, so his cottage will be available."

Faith looked at Gabe, and then spoke, "Yes, I'm sure we can do that."

"It's decided then," Maddy said.

Cooper made it official with the governor later that morning. Afterwards, he wrote a letter to Eli summarizing all that had taken place. He put it in Virgil Culpepper's capable hands and sent him back to Savannah with Buck Jewell. He explained that he'd return soon and that Maddy's parents would be coming as well. He also asked if 'Calico' had any meaning to Eli, outside of the long dead pirate captain, John Rackham, also known as Calico Jack. He'd been hung in 1720. The pirate's nickname came from the fancy clothing that he wore. Was that similarity a clue? One could only wonder.

* * *

HMS Minotaur led Admiral Davy's squadron into English Harbour with cannons booming out salutes. *SeaFire* stood out to sea with the American flag flying overhead as the British squadron sailed into port.

"I still get a case of the nerves when we get that close to a British warship," Buck Jewell volunteered to Virgil.

"Aye, it will pucker your arse for sure."

They both laughed, but they also knew that it would take the resources of both countries to put a stop to these new Brethren of the Coast.

CHAPTER TEN

VICE ADMIRAL RETIRED SIR Gabriel Anthony rode in the coach with his son-in-law, Cooper Cain. A man that he'd come to like, but more importantly...respect. They were headed down to the water at English Harbour where a barge would be waiting to take them to the seventy-four gun ship of the line, *Minotaur*. His old flag captain was now a rear admiral, and his son the flag captain.

His son was named after the man who sat beside Gabe, his old cox'n, Jake. The boy had the sea bred into him by his father, uncle, and grandfather and namesake. Gabe's reverie was suddenly broke by Cooper.

Cooper, with his head out the door, yelled for the driver to stop. Once the coach stopped, Cooper was out the door and running. "T...T Brim," he yelled.

The man, hearing his name, stopped and turned. It was not the name he used now. It was a name from years ago when he was the quartermaster of the *Tigre*, Dominique Youx's ship. T was not sure if he needed to run or prepare to defend himself. But damme, the fellow had a smile on his and looked familiar.

Cooper, seeing the man's scowl, shouted, "T, its Cooper Cain, from the *Raven*."

"T's scowl turned into a smile. He remembered and recognized that name...Cooper Cain. He was all dressed up in finery and riding in a fancy coach. T thought life had been good to the former pirate, much better that it had been to him. It was no one's fault but T's. Money had been plentiful and easy to get. He had spent it as his brethren had, on women and the games. He was now looking for a ship to sign on with just to have food and a hammock.

Cooper noted the shabbiness of Brim's attire as he walked up. "How are you, old friend?"

"Main well, just looking for a ship," T replied.

"You've no place to be?" Cooper asked.

"No."

Cooper took out his purse and dug out a guinea, the only English coin he had. "Yonder is a pub. Treat yourself until I return. I have a need for you, if you've a mind to join me after we talk."

Brim made to hand the coin back. "I'll wait."

"Nonsense you keep it," Cooper said. "We were once brethren."

Brim nodded his head and said again, "I'll wait."

"You won't be sorry," Cooper said and rushed back to the coach.

"Who was that?" Gabe asked.

"A face from the past," Cooper responded. "He is as capable a man as you'd want on your side and as deadly an enemy as walks. A good omen, I'd say."

Gabe nodded and thought, *so another rogue walks the streets of English Harbour*. Maybe this rogue would be on their side.

***

FULL HONORS WERE RENDERED for Sir Gabe, retired or not, as he went on board *Minotaur*. His son stood there beaming, pride in his new position and command. Rear Admiral David Davy stood next to Jake, and slightly behind him was Ariel.

Greeting Admiral Davy, Gabe embraced Ariel, "Dagan is here."

"Wonderful," the girl said. "I can't wait to see him."

Cooper came through the entry port. Captain Jake Anthony was glad to see his brother-in-law and greeted him warmly.

Admiral Davy couldn't help but remember Cooper Cain as 'Sir Pirate'. He found it hard not to like the man, but still there was something between them. Something he had yet to identify. But if Sir Gabe liked him, it was good enough for him...for now.

Admiral Davy's captains were already waiting in his cabin. He entered, followed by Gabe, Cooper, Captain Jake Anthony, and Jake Hex, Sir Gabe's cox'n. The captains stood up as their admiral and the others showed up.

Davy introduced Sir Gabe and let Gabe introduce Cooper. "Gentlemen, I want to introduce you to the rogue who stole my daughter, and your flag captain's sister's heart. He is now my son-in-law. His past is somewhat colorful, as he was a pirate previously. He has been referred to as 'Sir Pirate'. He did me a great service, however, as he attacked a pirate camp and freed my wife and daughter and saved our governor's life. He had to make a choice, so he chose to give up pirating and received a pardon from the King. I tell you this so that you know the man who speaks to you, speaks from experience. I also want you to know that I've come to respect this man and consider him a dear friend. I trust that you will look at him in the same light. Gentlemen, I present Cooper Cain."

If the captains were shocked, they didn't show it. Most of them were young, and three were in their first commands. Young captains with fresh, new ideas, and that was just what was needed. The old line of battle was a thing of the past, and was out of place for the work at hand.

Cooper came to the head of the table. He had prepared some notes...things that he and Dagan had gone over. He sat the list on the table and subconsciously rubbed the scar on his face.

Gabe recognized it for what it was. How many times had he rubbed the side of his head where a ball had creased his scalp? While the rest of his hair had been black, the crease had turned his hair white along the length of it. It was hardly recognizable now with all the gray hair he had. But he'd not forgotten how it had got there, nor would Cooper Cain.

"Thank you, Sir Gabe," Cooper began. "I've been asked to assume the position as pirate hunter by Sir Robert Basnight. It was he and Sir Gabe…along with Lloyds of London I'm told, who are responsible for the assembly of this squadron to rid the pirates from these waters, so our merchant ships can ply their trade. Catching a pirate is mostly luck. They have no allegiance to anyone other than themselves. They may be loosely tied to a consortium but that's all. There are a few things that are a 'must', however. Without them, there'd be no pirates. First, they need a reliable base of operation, a place where they can feel somewhat safe and be able to relax between voyages. You will need to look for a safe harbour. It will not be Saint Johns, Bermuda, or such places. It won't be San Juan either, but it might be like the island of Culebra. An island with a safe protected anchorage and fairly close to an island where they can be supplied. I'm talking about food, drink, and women. Without the three of them, you couldn't keep a crew around very long."

"You'd need to be close to a place that could supply ship materials next. Pirate ships never have enough. They get some from the ships that they capture but those are a chancy thing, so you'd need to have access to shipping materials. Just like with the Navy or a private shipping company, a ship must be kept ready for sea. Pirates must also have weapons. Rarely does a merchant ship have more than a cursory means of defense, so this offers very little to a pirate ship's armament. We need to know who is selling weapons and keep a watch on them. The last two items go hand in hand. A pirate needs a means of turning plunder into coin. They need a place where captured slaves can be sold. These are places like Cuba, New Orleans, Savannah, and Charleston. A person of value can be ransomed back to his or her family. There are people who will act as intermediaries and they usually do this to prevent death…or in the case of young women and girls, a fate worse than death. They are usually the last link in a chain so tracing the pirate back down the chain is useless but getting a captive back may provide useful information."

"A question."

"Yes, Captain Anthony," Cooper replied.

"Is there a profit for the intermediary?"

"Yes, it's usually paid by the captive or captive's family."

"Lastly, what do the pirates do with the loot they plunder from the merchant ships?" Anthony asked.

"Most pirates have clandestine contacts, which take the goods of little value to the pirates, but have great value on the market. Jean LaFitte was such a man. He had a steady flow of customers willing to buy slaves, bolts of cloth, spices, sugar, cocoa, tobacco, and the finer spirits." Cooper paused a moment, and then continued, "Unless Dagan has more to add, I think that other than working out the actual protocols and operations that will about get it. Dagan…"

Dagan raised slowly, his joints stiff from sitting through Coop's presentation. There was not a man at the table who hadn't at least heard the stories of Vice Admiral Sir Gabriel's uncle and confidant. They'd also heard of his power to see things and how men who crossed him often died through unexplainable circumstances. But the stories were from long ago. Did the old salt still have it in him?

"Calico…" Dagan said. "Calico to some brings back the memories of the pirate Calico Jack. He was named so because of his dress. To me, it brings images of a "dandy." Being a dandy doesn't mean the man is not without cunning or cruelty. He is a man of means, or at least he had the means at some point, also a man who is aware of the ways of society, and the men of society. I think while there may be several ships sailing under the black flag, there is only one leader. One man who has set up a company, a fiefdom of pirates. That means every rogue captured needs to be questioned at length, each individual separately. But never ask directly about Calico. Let the man speak and have a record of what they say written down. That way we may be able to get a clear picture of what and who we are dealing with."

Dagan sat down. He didn't say that he had a nagging feeling that Calico was a man or a person from the past. He needed to get by himself, and find a place, possibly at sea where he could meditate and hopefully awaken the old spirits that talked to him. How many times had he lain down awake and wondered if his ability was a gift or a curse? Betsy had eased his mind saying that it was a special gift…a gift that could only come from above. Betsy…gone now, but never from his heart or mind. They'd had a special love, a rare love. He often wondered, as he did now, how long must he endure before he would leave this earth to be with her. It was still a while yet. He'd seen that in a dream. He was playing with Maddy and Coop's son. Yes, they'd have a son, but he hadn't and wouldn't tell. Maddy could feel it, he knew that. Women often did. Well, that was for tomorrow.

Men…sea captains were coming to him now. They would have questions. Humm! His opinion and insight was suddenly needed again. Maybe the gift was awakening with this sudden need, this crisis. Dagan reached out and shook the offered hand. A boy captain, much as Gabe had been. A quick glance and he saw that Gabe was looking at him. A knowing nod passed between them. Like the old days…just like the old days.

CHAPTER ELEVEN

TBRIM SAT IN THE Ship's Anchor tavern. He'd nursed his rum along from recent habit. Money had been short and hard to come by. But there in front of him was the change from a guinea. He could have had as many tankards as he desired. He raised his hand to a serving wench, indicating another round, and she came right over with a fresh drink. He paid for it and slipped a shilling between her breasts. A huge smile appeared on the woman's face. A closer look revealed that she was older than she looked and she had tiny stretch marks along the side of her breasts which indicated a child or at least a pregnancy. If she was working at a tavern catering to seamen, her life must undoubtedly be tough.

The door opened, letting the sun's bright light enter the tavern and causing Brim to squint and the wench to put her hand over her eyes. A well dressed gent walked in and sidled up to the customer she'd just served. No wonder he could afford to tip a shilling and not ask for favors. The gent looked like a man of means but seemed perfectly at home in a seaman's tavern.

✱✱✱

COOPER SHOOK HANDS WITH T and made small talk for a few minutes. He then ordered cold meat, cheese, bread, and a pint. Once the order was delivered, Cooper came to the point. "I need a man like you, T." You will be my first officer if you agree. You will get the same pay as would a first officer on a privateer, only…we aren't going after merchant ships."

Cooper paused waiting on Brim to ask the obvious, "What are we hunting?"

"Pirates!" Cooper replied.

"Pirates!?" T repeated.

"Aye, the day of the pirate is past. The new breed is worse than we ever were. Besides, if we capture a friend, they have a better chance of surviving with us than somebody else. England and our country are both making a concerted effort to rid the seas of pirates. Eli Taylor and I are partners in a shipping business. Men who sailed with us under the black flag, or as privateers with me, have all been offered jobs paying far more than they ever earned pirating. You remember Johannes Ewers? He is master of a company ship. He had to fight for his life recently. Damn pirates attacked the wrong ship though, when they attacked Johannes. What I'm offering you, T, is employment with me until the pirates have been purged from the sea and then with our company for as long as you desire."

"I know nothing of merchant ships," T Brim said.

"You know ships and you know the sea. The rest will come easy." Cooper asked the serving girl for a writing quill, ink, and paper.

When she brought it, he slipped her another shilling. He wrote down an address and gave T another guinea. "Think on it. If you decide to come along, come to this address tomorrow by 10:00 A.M. Bring your chest with you." Brim nodded, but he didn't mention that there was no chest to bring. Looking at the note, it said Sir Gabe Anthony's house with the address beneath. Cooper had come up in the world, he decided.

T finished off his rum and called the girl over to him. "What's your name?"

"Dolcie."

"Do you have a place nearby?"

"Yes...but I'm not a doxy," she said.

"I didn't think you were," Brim replied. "I've had a change of luck and plans. I need a place to stay tonight. I'll pay for the night, more if breakfast is included."

"That's all?" Dolcie asked.

"A cot and maybe a meal, nothing else," he said.

"I live on the side of the hill. It's a small place but there's a cot and I'll fix you breakfast."

T nodded his head and said, "For that I'll pay you three shillings."

"Oh, that's too much. I only pay five shillings a week," she said.

"How much do you make working here?" Brim asked.

"Six shillings a week and I keep half the tips."

"Half?" Brim exclaimed.

"Yes," Dolcie replied.

T stood and walked over to the man behind the bar. "Is this your place?"

"Aye."

"Do you know who the Anthonys are?"

"Aye, who doesn't," the bartender said.

"I'm going to be doing some work for them, so I'll be in and out of here for the next year."

"I'll be glad to serve you."

Brim looked at the bartender and said, "You'll do more than that. From now on you'll pay Dolcie seven shillings a week and she'll keep all her tips." The man flushed but didn't speak. Brim continued, "If I find out that she's not been treated well, then this conversation will get personal like."

"I don't take to..." The sentence was never finished as eight inches of cold steel was pressed against the tavern owner's throat. A thin red line appeared and started to trickle down the man's neck.

"Do we understand each other?" Brim asked.

The man gave a brief nod. T took the blade away and wiped it on a bar towel. "Put some gin on your neck so that it doesn't fester." The man nodded but didn't move. "Do it," Brim said firmly.

Turning to Dolcie, Brim asked, "What time do you get off?"

"At four o'clock," she said.

"That's another hour, so I'll be back."

"I'll be here," Dolcie said, speaking softly, the hint of a smile on her lips.

T had roughly twenty shillings left. He'd pay Dolcie three shillings for the bed and breakfast so he'd have roughly fifteen shillings to spend on clothes. He'd seen a store with used clothes down the street. He'd see what he could find there. He didn't want to show up at Coop's without a bath and in the same clothes.

He thought then about what he'd done at the tavern, dropping the Anthony name as he had. Undoubtedly, it carried a degree of weight on the island. He didn't fully understand Coop's relationship with the family but it must be close for him to be traveling around in a crested carriage.

Coker and Baldwin Slop Sellers was the store T went to. He bought a better pair of shoes, a pair of stockings, two speckled shirts, and two pair of britches. He saw a hat hut didn't add it. The shopkeeper came up with a price of twenty-one shillings.

T looked awed, "I could buy it all for ten shillings at home." He didn't say where home was.

"This is an island. Things are much more expensive here," the clerk reminded him.

"They are used, not new," T threw back. He then set the clothes back down and made to leave.

"Fifteen shillings is as low as I can go," the clerk said.

Brim paused and then turned around. He picked up the hat and set it on the pile. "Fifteen shillings for it all, and not a farthing more," he said.

The clerk seemed to ponder the sale so T started toward the door. "Fifteen shillings it is, but don't tell a soul what you paid for it or I'm out of a job."

Brim smiled, "Even with the hat, you still will make three to five shillings profit, maybe more. " The clerk wrapped up T's packages and he left.

He was back at the tavern a little after four o' clock, and Dolcie was waiting outside for him. She said, "Don't go back in there. He has two of his men in there waiting on you."

"Is that a fact?" T asked, reaching for the door.

"Please don't go in," Dolcie said.

T could see the fear on the woman's face so he relented. It was a good walk uphill to Dolcie's little cottage. *Shack was more like it*, Brim thought, but didn't say it. By the time they were there, T's shirt was wringing wet as his mother used to say.

The place was neat, once they were inside. He didn't see a child so maybe he had been wrong and hadn't seen the stretch marks on Dolcie's breasts. He looked at her, and not wanting to be impolite, he said, "Not bad. It's small, but for only one or two, it will certainly do."

"There's only me. My husband and baby died from the fever," Dolcie replied.

"I'm sorry, I didn't mean to pry."

Dolcie looked at T's clothes. "Those clothes need washing and you need a bath. I have a tub, believe it or not. I'll heat some water up for you."

"You have a well?" he asked.

"Cistern, we don't drink from it, but it's okay to wash and clean with."

Dolcie put a pot of water on a hook and started a fire. She carried a pot of cold water into the small room. A blanket was used to partition the room off from the main room. She went back for another pot of water. T took the pot then went back and got another one.

"Take off your clothes while I get you some soap and a towel," she said.

T, doing as he was told, climbed in the tub. Dolcie returned with the heated water and said, "It's not too hot, but you better stand while I pour it in the tub." When he paused, Dolcie said, "Don't be shy, I've been married and I grew up with brothers."

Once the heated water was poured in, T eased down into the tub. Dolcie took a cloth and with the soap she lathered it up good.

"It has been a long time since I've washed a man's back," she said. "In fact, it has been a long time since I've touched a man at all."

T took her hand from his shoulder and pulled her around to face him. "I'm not sure how long I will be on the island. I'm signing on a ship tomorrow. After that, I can't say."

Dolcie stood up and unbuttoned her top, "There's no time to waste then, is there?"

"No," he replied, and then he added, "I'm Talley Brim, but most people just call me T."

"I'm Dolcie Hart," she whispered as her lips met his and he pulled her into the small tub, splashing water onto the rough plank floor.

They bathed each other and explored each other's bodies, as they kissed. Dolcie had a hunger that was easy for T to recognize. He did his best to quench her desires and when, at last, she collapsed in his arms, he made a vow. He'd get a better place for Dolcie. She'd not go back to that tavern if he could help it.

CHAPTER TWELVE

S IR ROBERT MET WITH Cooper that evening. "We have the ship that I think you'll need, Cooper. She's much like *SeaFire*, but with better armament. She arrived today under the temporary command of a lieutenant."

"I didn't know a governor could order a ship," Coop said smiling.

"I can't, but with a few well placed words here and there, I'm generally able to get what is needed when the benefit is felt in a man's purse. Besides, when this pirate business is finished, she will likely become some young officer's first command."

"When do I get to see her?" Cooper asked.

"How about tomorrow, say around one o' clock," Sir Robert replied.

"One it is," Cooper said.

After a few more minutes with the governor, Coop then made his way back to Gabe and Faith's house. Quang fell in with him, once he left the governor's house. Getting into the waiting coach, Cooper thought back to several years ago when he'd rescued Maddy, Faith, Sir Robert, and the others. During the passage to Antigua, he, Mac, and Johannes had explained what type of ship he would like to have to make the perfect raider. Mac and Johannes had added a lot to the theory. A fast sailor, a shallow draught to get into places a larger ship couldn't, well armed to protect it but not so much as to weigh her down or slow her down, berthing for a crew of one hundred twenty to one hundred thirty-five men, but very little hold space. If the operation was successful, the number of crewmen would dwindle with each prize taken and so would the need for supplies.

Little did Cooper ever suspect Sir Robert was making more of the comments beyond polite conversation. Tomorrow he'd see Sir Robert's raider, but tonight he wanted to get home to Maddy.

"Did you find T?" Cooper asked Quang.

"Yes, he had words with the tavern keeper over girl, then he leave. He bought clothes and then he go back to tavern. Girl was waiting outside the tavern for him. Tavern keeper big mad, he hires men to beat T, but girl beg T not to fight, so he go to her house. Lights soon out so me come back here." Quang's broken English was improving.

Coop understood Quang and was able to form a picture of what his Chinaman cox'n had told him. He fully expected T to be here at ten o'clock tomorrow morning, but if the tavern keeper was after him, maybe he should send Quang and Ox over to help out if the need arose.

"Do you know where Ox or Spurlock are, Quang?"

"At Bart's place," Quang replied.

Cooper couldn't help but smile. He'd learned Lord Anthony's friend and one time cox'n was an expert card player…not just an expert card player but a man of repute. He owned a nice tavern. It wasn't a seaman's dive but one for Antigua's upper crust. In fact, he owned one over on Saint Johns, as well.

Coop looked at Quang and said, "I'll have the coach take you to Bart's tavern. You explain to Ox or any of our men who are there what's happened and let them know I don't want any harm to come to T or his lady."

Quang shook his head as was his usual. He only spoke when a nod or a shake of his head wouldn't do. Occasionally, he'd say, 'shi' or 'hui' for yes and 'bu shi' or 'bu hui' for no. Eli had said there was no quick Chinese translation for no, so just know that bu shi or bu hui meant a negative. Coop and Quang communicated well enough that they could understand one another and that's all that mattered.

Everyone was still up when Coop got home. He'd told Gabe about the ship, and from his reply Coop got the feeling that he already knew about it. Coop wondered if the governor had thought to inform David Davy about it. Coop was at a loss as he was not sure.

"If you'd like, Coop, I know Admiral Davy is having dinner with Ariel and Dagan. We can send Jake over with an invitation or we could ride over ourselves. Dinner is still an hour away."

Coop understood that Gabe was telling him to do all in his power to make sure that he maintained a good relationship with the man he was to depend on for support. "I think that a personal invitation would hold more weight, don't you?"

Gabe smiled at his son-in-law and said, "That was my thinking but it had to be your choice."

Gabe and Cooper told their wives that they were stepping out for a while. As their husbands left, Maddy said to her mother, "Is father still upset that I married Cooper?"

Faith took her daughter in her arms. "No man would be good enough for you in your father's eyes. Having said that though, he's fond of Cooper. More than once during this last war, he's put a young, full of himself captain in his place by telling him that his son-in-law was making a mockery of the Royal Navy as a privateer and, until three years ago, he'd never set foot on board a ship. He said it with a sense of pride, Jake told me. So don't you worry, Maddy, they left here like conspirators."

❋ ❋ ❋

T AND DOLCIE, SPENT from their passion, fell asleep. He was holding Dolcie when he was awakened. It was not the usual gradual awakening after two people had filled each other's desires. It was a sudden jolt, and was like a loud thud. Something slammed against the side of the cottage. Whatever it was, it woke both T and Dolcie with a start. The two of them looked at one another for only a moment when T reached for his britches. He'd lived with danger too long to believe it was nothing. After his britches were on, he slipped on his shoes.

"Do you have a pistol here?" he asked.

"No," Dolcie replied.

T reached for his blade. He'd have liked to have had a pistol, but you used what you had. He made his way into the main room. The door was latched but it wasn't meant to keep anything out beyond a strong wind. T, seeing a kitchen knife, picked it up. He now had a weapon for each hand.

Voices were heard as men whispered to each other…drunken voices. "Do we go in?"

"We will if he doesn't come out," one of the two men said. "We were told to rough 'em up."

"If we go in, somebody is likely to die," a third man said. "Hit the bloody wall with the plank again."

"There's no need to do that," T said as he stepped out of the cottage door.

The three men looked, somewhat startled by his sudden appearance and calm demeanor. "Now, I want one of you to tell me who sent you, while you can still talk."

"Yer bloody daff, there's three of us."

T shook his head and struck, as the three men stared at him. His fist slammed into the throat of the first man. Spinning, he backhanded the second man. He missed the throat but the backhanded slap made the man see stars. T kicked at the groin of the third man, who moved back just enough so that T's foot missed its mark. It landed against the rogue's knee instead. The loud crack of the bone was heard only a split second before the man's screams broke the evening's peaceful silence. The first man was still trying to catch a breath and holding his throat. The second man, however, had cleared his head and pulled a pistol.

"Back away," he said, "or I'll…"

The sentence was never finished as a large meaty hand grabbed the rogue. The hand clamped down on the wrist like a vise. The rogue's hand went numb and the pistol fell from his hand. Spurlock looked at the man's hand. It was visibly white where Ox had gripped it so tight that he'd cut off the blood supply.

"Turn loose the whoreson, Ox," Spurlock said. When the blood rushed back into the man's hand, he grimaced and bent over in pain.

"Hurts don't it," Spurlock said with a smile. "It's worse if he squeezes your head, but that's better than death. Do you see the blade in the man's hand?" Spurlock asked. "Before you could have aimed and pulled the trigger that knife would have entered yer skull about here." Spurlock jabbed the man between the eyes twice, his fingernail breaking the skin each time. A trickle of blood ran down onto the rogue's nose and face, and Spurlock spoke again. "Gather yer mates and be gone." Two of the men got an arm under their mate with the broken leg and left.

Spurlock turned to his friend. "T! It's a mess you were in."

"Aye, and it's a killing you stopped, to be sure," T replied.

Dolcie, now dressed, stepped outside the cottage door.

"These are friends of mine," T said and introduced Spurlock, Ox, and Quang. "I don't know this man," he said.

"This is Coop's sharpshooter. His name is Spurlin," Ox offered. "He can shoot the eye out of a hog at fifty yards."

"That's some shooting," T said.

"Pure fact, it is," Spurlock said.

"How did you men happen to show up here?" T asked.

"Quang overheard the tavern keeper plotting to get you, so he came to get us."

T nodded, "I was wondering if Coop was protecting his investment."

"Well, Quang was sent to keep watch," Spurlock replied.

T smiled, "I'd offer you a drink but alas." He held his hands out to the side indicating that there was none.

"Not to worry," Spurlock said. "We'll catch you later."

"Should one of us stay close by?" Ox asked as the men made ready to go.

"Me stay," Quang volunteered.

They all shook hands again and everyone left. Quang walked over to a tree and sat down under it.

"Quang be good here," he said.

T and Dolcie went back inside the cottage.

CHAPTER THIRTEEN

QUANG AND T WERE at Gabe and Faith's house the next morning before ten.

"I'll join," T said, "but I'd like to borrow ten pounds up front."

"Sure," Cooper said. "Would I be out of place asking why?"

T told all that had gone on the previous evening, including how Dolcie lost her husband and baby. "I have to get her another place and give her enough to survive on until she can find work."

The women were in the room next door and overheard the conversation. Ann, Cooper's mother, came into the room the men were in. "I...we couldn't help but overhear the conversation," she began. "Jean Paul and I have an apartment here. We were thinking of hiring someone to keep it, when we are at the plantation. There's a storage room that can be made into a small bedroom and, of course, she can use the rest of the house. When we are there, she can cook for us but when we are gone, all she needs to do is keep the place clean. The pay wouldn't be much but it would include meals and a place to stay."

"It sounds perfect," T said, thanking Ann for her offer.

Cooper looked at T and said, "You and Quang take the carriage and go get her and her things. Pay off her rent and come back here. Mother will take her to the apartment. This afternoon we'll go down to the dockyard and see our new ship." He took out his purse and counted out fifteen pounds. "This is just in case you need a little extra," he said, as he handed the money to Brim.

✱✱✱

HMS STAG STOOD JUST off the shallow waters near the dockyard. She was a beautiful ship. She'd been laid down in 1795 but had just undergone a complete overhaul. She gleamed as the sun shone down on the fresh paint and new rigging. The stag figure-head jutted proudly from the bow, its hind legs extending to just above the cutwater.

Stag was one hundred and twenty feet long with a beam of only thirty-three feet. Her sail plan was that of a full-rigged ship. Cooper knew instantly that this ship would be the hunter. Her deck carried twenty-four twelve-pounder cannons. The quarterdeck carried six eighteen-pound carronades, with two more eighteen-pounder carronades on the forecastle.

Lieutenant Drury, who was in temporary command of *Stag*, was proud of the ship. It had been his job to sail her from Portsmouth to Antigua. Giving up the ship had to hurt, Cooper surmised, but the lieutenant put up a good front.

The lieutenant, speaking to Cooper, Admiral Davy, and Sir Gabe, explained, "The quarterdeck originally had four six-pounder guns. These were removed and two more of the carronades were installed. Two nine-pounder stern chasers were added. Someone also decided to add more swivel guns, so you have a total of twelve extra guns scattered about the ship. *Stag* could easily take on a thirty-six and maybe even a thirty-eight gun frigate, with the firepower that she has."

Cooper kept noticing that Admiral Davy was staring at the young lieutenant. "Tell me, Lieutenant Drury, don't I know you?" Davy finally asked.

"Yes sir, I was one of your midshipman when you were flag captain for Sir Gabe. I passed my lieutenant's exam and was sent to the *Cyclops* as a third lieutenant. I was first lieutenant on board the *Pearl* when the war ended. My captain recommended me for command. The port admiral, knowing I was from Saint John, recommended me as job captain, so here I am."

"Lieutenant Drury," Cooper called. "I need a man to be my second in command. A man experienced in the type of work that we will be doing. If you'd like the assignment and Admiral Davy agrees, I'd value you being my second lieutenant. I think that your experience on *Stag* would be a great help."

Sir Gabe winked at Cooper and Admiral Davy had the hint of a smile. Cooper had noticed the admiral rarely smiled when he was present. Something he'd like to see changed.

"Sir," Lieutenant Drury spoke, getting Cooper's attention.

"Yes, Lieutenant."

"Sir, I'd like to recommend Lieutenant Lewis Potts as the third lieutenant."

Cooper paused, "If you recommend him and the admiral agrees, I don't see why not."

❋❋❋

HMS Stag ONLY HAD a skeleton crew, just enough to sail her from England to Antigua. Therefore, the crew would need to be augmented. This was something that Cooper had expected. He, Johannes, and Virgil Culpepper sat down aboard *SeaFire* and worked out the list of crewman from the old days that each would carry. Spurlock, Diamond, Spurlin, Banty and Ox would go with Cooper. Of course, he'd also have Quang and Brim. Johannes would keep the rest. Both ships also needed doctors. Dagan was not mentioned but it was understood that he'd sail with Cooper. They'd ask for Lieutenant Lewis Potts, *Stag's* other lieutenant, to remain on board as the third lieutenant.

"Virgil, you deserve a ship. Should we get a prize, she will be yours."

Virgil waved off Cooper's comments. "There are no worries there, Captain."

When the meeting broke up, Cooper had the coach driver take him to the anchorage. He needed to talk with Admiral Davy. He would need another twenty men, but the important thing was to speak to Davy, man to man. They needed to clear the air between the two of them before the mission went any further. He hired a bumboat to take him to the ship. He was allowed on board by the duty lieutenant, who had sent for the captain.

Captain Jacob Anthony hurried to meet his brother-in-law. "Welcome back on board *Minotaur*," Captain Anthony said, shaking Cooper's hand and putting an arm over his shoulder as he led Cooper to his cabin.

The lieutenant on watch, along with a couple more lieutenants on deck, noted the warm greeting their captain gave this Cooper Cain, pirate, and now pirate hunter. Each of them decided that they'd be wise to show respect when dealing with the man.

Captain Anthony had been given open door policy when he needed to see the admiral. Today, he had the marine announce him. Cooper had been up front with Jake as to his reason for appearing on the flagship. As this might, at some point, affect his standing and relationship with Admiral Davy, he chose formality over the usual open door.

Admiral Davy looked up at Jake, and the usual smiling face was not there. Davy sensed that something unpleasant had happened or was about to happen. "Yes, Captain," Davy spoke in a formal tone.

"Captain Cain has come aboard requesting to talk with you, sir."

"Has he?" Davy smirked. "Send in our pirate friend, then."

Jake turned to leave and then stopped. He turned back to Admiral Davy who appeared agitated.

"Yes, Captain."

"May I speak freely, Admiral?"

"Yes, Jake. We've been friends too long for you not to when we are alone," Davy replied.

Jake took a breath and then took a step closer to where Davy was sitting. "I take offense to your comment, sir. He was a pirate, but he gave up the trade. He has saved my mother and sister's life twice. He saved Maddy from being raped. He saved Sir Robert Basnight's life as well. Our governor saw fit to apply to the King for a pardon which was justly given. He has married my sister with my mother and father's blessing. I could go on but I'll stop. However, he is my brother-in-law." Jake paused, thinking what would his father say or do.

Admiral Davy stood up and walked over to his desk and leaned on it. "Your brother-in-law turned his back on his country and continued to raid our ships in this past war. He may have possessed a Letter of Marque but in my book he is still a pirate and a traitor."

Jake was suddenly so mad that he was trembling. "A traitor," he spat out. "What about all of our captains and admirals who retired to keep from fighting? What about all those who carried on trade with the Colonies during the war. Are they not traitors? Yes, Cooper was a privateer. He was a man who, before he was cast away unjustly, had no idea what a ship was. But he quickly learned and put every Royal Navy captain to shame, including me. He was so good that we have called upon him to rid us of the sea wolves. In fact, if I may, Admiral, he was so good that Sir Robert and my father recommended him to be the hunter. It was my father who wrote numerous letters recommending you as the Navy commander to provide for this task. I may be out of line,

Admiral, but as you yourself have said, 'Father is the reason that you have your flag.' I wonder how he will feel when he hears of the contempt and disrespect you hold for his son-in-law."

Admiral Davy took a deep breath, "Is that all, Captain?"

"No sir, it isn't. I think that under the circumstances you should find yourself another flag captain."

Admiral Davy straightened up and walked back to his desk.

Jake spoke once more, "If there's nothing more, sir, I will attend to my duties."

Davy shook his head. He called to Jake as he was turning to go, "I know Captain Cain needs men, see that he gets them."

"Aye!"

"Tell Captain Cain that today is not a convenient time to talk. I will, however, talk with him soon."

"Aye, aye sir."

When Jake had left, Admiral Davy called his servant. When the man answered, Davy said, "Call my cox'n. I'm going ashore."

Jake relayed the admiral's message to Cooper, who thanked him and left.

***

A KNOCK AT THE door caused Maddy to put down the book that she was reading on childbirth and go answer the door. She was surprised to see David Davy standing there.

"Is you father home, Maddy?"

"Yes, come in," she said.

Gabe walked in with a smile on his face until he saw the grim look on Davy's. "Is everything alright, David?"

A hint of a smile creased David's face. "Can we go somewhere and talk? My coach is outside."

Gabe called, "Maddy, tell your mother that I'm stepping out for awhile. Oh, Maddy," Gabe added, "everything is alright." He kissed his daughter on the forehead and followed his friend out to the coach.

"George, drive out to the country," Davy said, instructing his driver. Once they were settled in and the coach was moving along, he started to talk. "Have you ever had a junior officer dress you down?" Before Gabe could speak, Davy told him what had happened.

When Davy finished, he said, "I apologize, sir. I wrongly, and have always felt that Cooper was an embarrassment to the Anthony name and reputation. It was my loyalty to you and Lord Anthony that made me feel as I did. I understand that Maddy fell for the man but there's no explaining love. Regardless, I have no doubts that it was you who was responsible for me raising my flag while I in return have insulted your family. I hope that you will forgive me and accept my apology."

Gabe remained silent for a while, long enough that Davy was about to speak again. "I must share some of the responsibility for your feelings, David. In the beginning, I called Cooper a rogue and made no secret about my feelings toward the man. When I realized that my daughter was in love with Cooper, it only worsened. I was glad when he left, and then he came back. I wish you could have seen the joy and excitement in my daughter when he walked into the tavern, where Bart's birthday party was being held. Faith asked me, later that week, what I thought about Cooper. I recall saying that I owed him for my wife and daughter's lives, twice over. So how was I supposed to feel, rogue though he may be. She said, 'If you love your daughter you better find it in your heart to like him.' I remember looking at her and Faith telling me, 'He will be your son-in-law.' The more that I was around the boy, the more I come to realize how much I respected him. I didn't approve of his life and told him so. I remember asking him, an educated young man, if he thought it was fair to subject Maddy to the type of life that he lived. He told me right up that it wasn't and he'd give up the free trade. David, I've referred to him in unpleasant terms, at times, in front of you so some of your feelings came from me. I apologize and I owe Cooper an explanation and an apology. There's nothing to worry about though, it's Jake that we both need to talk to."

"No, Gabe, this is between Jake and me. No senior officer has a right to speak unkindly about a man's family. Do you recall how I reacted as a middy when Witz spoke unkindly about my mother?"

Gabe smiled remembering how little David Davy had bloodied Witz's nose.

"I'm just lucky that Jake didn't seek satisfaction," Davy said.

Davy returned to HMS *Minotaur* after dropping Gabe off at his home. Upon returning, Davy asked the watch officer to let the captain know that he'd like to see him when it was convenient. Jake reported immediately. He was still rigid and had a stern look on his face.

Davy smiled, trying to ease the situation, and called him by name. "Jake, I'm sorry. I was wrong. I apologize and I ask for your forgiveness."

Jake smiled and sat down, as was his usual. "Do you still want me as your flag captain?"

Admiral Davy smiled and said, "Nobody else would stand up to their admiral when he was wrong. I don't need a boot licker, Jake. I need a man to be my flag captain."

"Thank you, sir."

"No. Thank you, Jake," Davy replied.

CHAPTER FOURTEEN

NEEDHAMS POINT WAS VISIBLE and then it wasn't. When the rain slacked up, it became visible again. Cooper Cain had no intention of trying to enter Carlisle Bay in this weather. The rain had started at midday. Cooper's skin felt raw where the wind and rain whipped at the exposed areas. He had no complaints, other than the weather. His ship, that was how he thought of HMS *Stag*, was a remarkable sailor. Until the weather had made it necessary to take in a few sails, the ship's master had felt that they'd set a record for the time that it took to sail from English Harbour to Barbados. Of course, God ruled the seas and elements, not man, so if it was his will to throw a squall at them, then all they could do was meet the challenge the best way they could.

"This is better than a drill," Brim had remarked.

Men often slacked off in a drill, yet when their lives were on the line the real picture and worth of a man presented itself. T and Lieutenant Drury compared notes on each man's strengths and weaknesses and made changes so that two weak men would not be on the same watch but teamed up with men who had strength and experience.

Brisco, the sailing master, also paid attention to the two master's mates and kept notes on the two midshipmen. The older one, Midshipman Short, should have been made a lieutenant a long time ago. He'd make cannon fodder but is worth little else, Brisco had told Captain Cain. He had as yet shown the master anything of which would create confidence. The younger midshipman, Mr. Shirreffs, though, had a deal of promise. Cooper had never dealt with midshipmen, so he left their training to the master and Lieutenant Drury.

The rain continued another hour and then stopped. The men had missed their midday meal so the galley fires were lit to give the men a hot meal.

Cooper went down to his cabin followed by Quang. Josiah had a snifter of brandy ready for Cooper. Quang rarely drank but he downed the glass that Josiah handed to him in a single gulp. A knock at the door and the marine announced Lieutenant Drury. Having a detachment of marines on board was something new to Cooper, and was at times distracting. He'd considered doing away with the practice, but Jake had told him that it was tradition and stopping it would be considered an insult to the marines. Cooper was finding it easier to get used to than he thought possible, and if it kept the tradition alive he was all for it.

"Evening, Captain. It's almost sunset and the weather caused the men to miss their noon rum issue. Therefore, if the captain agrees, now would be a good time to pass up spirits."

Agreeing, Cooper smiled. On board his previous ships this was understood at the scheduled times. The only time he was involved was when it was to be delayed or that special occasion when he wished to reward the men. The skylight was open so Cooper heard the men cheer when Lieutenant Drury ordered 'up spirits', splice the main brace.

Cooper, still smiling, called to Josiah, "I think another brandy would be good."

✳✳✳

IT WAS A MONTH since Cooper had taken HMS *Stag* out for the first time. After returning to English Harbour, he and Maddy had been the guests of Admiral Davy and Ariel. The change in the admiral was significant. So much so that Cooper was glad that he hadn't confronted the man.

After dining with the admiral and his wife, the following day they had sailed to Georgia. HMS *Stag* led the way out of the anchorage, followed by HMS *Syren*, a thirty-two gun frigate commanded by Captain Marcus Lanning. Two brigs, the *Swallow* of sixteen guns commanded by Lieutenant Van Ludlow, and the *Swan*, a brig of fourteen guns commanded by Lieutenant Daniel Dyea, followed them out of the harbour. The brigs were chosen as they could get into places the *Syren* and *Stag* couldn't. The two lieutenants, at the last meeting aboard the flagship, seemed very excited to be joining Cooper on the hunt.

After the meeting was over, the two lieutenants hung around almost an hour plying Cooper with one question after another. Jake Anthony finally sent them away.

Captain Marcus Lanning seemed a capable man. He had won...or maybe lost at drawing straws with the other frigate captains, to see who went with Cooper and who stayed and patrolled the Leeward Islands to the Virgin Islands.

This area had been hit but not like the Gulf of Mexico and the Bahamas. The islands around Puerto Rico, Hispaniola, and Cuba, as well as the Florida Keys would all be Cooper's responsibility to patrol. First, though, he would take Maddy and her parents to Georgia.

When Cooper and Maddy had returned home from the Davy's house, Maddy had been like a tigress in bed. "You seem to be on fire with desire tonight," Cooper said, when Maddy awakened him.

"We can't make love on board the ship," she said, "so I'm making up for lost time, in advance."

Cooper smiled, *God how I love this woman.* Only she would think of making up for lost time in advance.

***

THEY WERE ABOUT A day from the Georgia coast when the lookout spotted a wreck. It was Banty at the mainmast. No one else could see it, and after a time Lieutenant Drury began to wonder if he'd really spotted anything.

"If Banty said he saw something," Brim said, "he did. It may have sunk since he spotted her, but it was there."

Cooper was about to go up when Banty called down again. This time, though, Midshipman Short saw it as well.

"Off to larboard, almost to midship," Banty called down. "She be low in the water."

Cooper climbed up in the shrouds and looked. He saw it, a merchant ship low in the water, but there were people on deck.

Brim sang out, "I see her, Captain. Shall we alter course to intercept her?"

"Aye," Coop replied, "I just hope we are not too late."

The main deck was nearly awash when *Stag* came alongside. Six people were on the deck; the captain, second mate, a man in his thirties, two children, and a black woman, who was the children's nanny.

"They took my wife," the father cried.

"They took all the women," the captain said.

"How old were they?" Cooper asked.

"Two girls about twelve or thirteen years old," the captain replied. "They also took two young women in their twenties. They killed one of the women's father and the other's husband, along with a young woman."

"She was twenty-four," the father added.

"We were carrying passengers from Charleston to New Orleans," the captain said. "The rogue captain said that hopefully they'd get enough for the women to make up for the loss in cargo. We fought until most of the crew was dead. After they took the women, the rogue captain spoke to a man in a bright suit. He wore a bright green hat, but over the hat, he had a veil, almost like a wedding veil. He also had a cane with a silver tip. He pointed the tip of the cane at us and the ship fired into our hull. It was like he almost wanted us to suffer."

"How long ago was this?"

"Two hours," the captain said.

"Which way did they head?"

"Southerly, like they were headed to Florida," the captain replied.

The Navy ships were standing off. Cooper signaled for them to close. Once in hailing distance, Cooper summarized what had happened and sent the *Syren* and *Swallow* to try to find the cut-throats. If they hadn't spotted the ship by midnight, they were to come about and head to Savannah.

CHAPTER FIFTEEN

T RODE OUT TO COOPER's farm, at his invitation. He sat next to Quang on the wagon seat. The back of the wagon was loaded down with luggage. The countryside was quiet and beautiful. T thought to himself that he wouldn't mind having a place like this when he could. The offer from Cooper had come along at the right time. He'd made his purchases of the things that he'd need aboard ship and had given the rest to Dolcie. They had made love off and on most of the last night he was ashore. She had promised there would be no others until he returned, even though it was not clear when that might be. *Could he be happy with Dolcie?* He had been during the time that they were together, but that was only a short time. Cooper seemed happy enough. Of course, he'd married the daughter of a sailing man, so she knew what it was like to be alone for long periods of times. *Could Dolcie do that?* He'd find out.

"Here gate," Quang said.

It was a nice entrance but nothing fancy, like the man who owned it, T thought. As they rode along, T picked out the river flowing alongside of them. He saw the little fenced in grave, and tapped Quang on the shoulder and pointed. "Who's grave?"

"Cap'n's first wife, Sophia," Quang replied in his broken English.

Hmm, T thought. Cooper had been married twice. Try as he might, he couldn't remember hearing anything about it.

Quang pointed then and said, "Dagan's house and the big house."

Looking about, T saw how well-organized the place was. *Damn Coop*, he thought. It would be hard for me to turn all this aside to hunt some hellish pirates. A number of people were walking out to greet Coop and Maddy.

"Slaves?" T asked.

Quang shook his head, "No slaves. Cap'n doesn't want slaves."

Recalling the number of slaves that Eli and Cooper had sold in New Orleans, T thought, *Cooper had made some changes. Was it his wife who'd brought about such changes?*

Rosa rushed up to Maddy, "I sho' been worried bout you, gal. It does my old heart good to see you home, so's I can take care o' you."

Faith walked up smiling and said, "Another Nanny."

Maddy hugged Rosa and replied, "Absolutely."

After everyone was settled in, Luke, Cooper's overseer, said, "Looks like we either need to add on or build a new house."

"I think build another house, Luke, near the bluff where Maddy likes to sit and watch the river."

"I know the spot," Luke responded.

"I will be going back to sea for awhile, Luke. Maddy's parents are going to live here while I'm gone. Work out the plans with Maddy. My only input is to have a deck off of our bedroom."

"It will be done, sir. How big should the house be, and how much do I spend on it?" Luke asked.

"I don't want to go broke building it, but Maddy is levelhead-ed when it comes to money. More than I am. I do want you to remember one thing, Luke. Maddy's father was a vice admiral in the Navy, and that's almost to the top of the chain. He has a tendency to speak like he's still in command at times. Don't let it bother you. Be polite, but do things as you know they're supposed to be done."

"Aye, Cap'n," Luke said, mimicking a sailor and causing both of them to laugh.

***

THE SHIPS WERE REPLENISHED over the next week, while a somewhat nervous Savannah community put out the welcome mat for the British Navy. It was hard to believe that less than two years ago Fort James Jackson was used to prevent the British from entering the city via the river. A meeting of the ships' captains, first lieutenants, and masters was held at the River Inn Restaurant. Johannes and Virgil were introduced to the British officers. Everyone seemed cordial and pleasant. However, Captain Lanning offered little beyond how the patrols would be set up and who would be the senior officer or officer in charge.

"For experience sake, Johannes and I will be in charge of each patrol," Cooper advised. "We will start out with *SeaFire* teamed up with *Swallow*, and *Stag* will patrol with *Swan*. Because of Captain Lannings' firepower, I thought that he could cruise independently down the coast of Florida and into the Gulf of Mexico, to New Orleans and back. We will set a rendezvous date and locations, with alternate dates and locations, in case a ship is unable to make the first rendezvous. We will stay at each rendezvous for three days. Captain Lanning, one of our ships will be going to New Orleans on the morrow. It will be taking the survivors from the wrecked ship that we picked up with them. Since that will be in your patrol area, I would like it if you gave them escort."

"As you wish, sir." The remark was very formal and stiff.

When the meeting broke up, most of the men headed to an empty table in the tavern part of the inn. Several young tavern wenches were glad to make their acquaintance. The men had all been warned not to discuss their mission with anyone. The ships' crews had not even been told exactly what they would be doing. Cooper had called his entire crew together at the warehouse of the Savannah Import/Export Company and explained the sensitive nature of their task. They were asked to keep their eyes on the British sailors. There was little doubt that Calico would have paid spies in most of the port cities.

Cooper spoke with Dagan and Gabe after the meeting. Of course, Gabe's cox'n, Jake, was there as well. "I get the feeling, Sir Gabe, that Captain Lanning is not thrilled with his assignment."

"I noticed it also," Gabe replied.

"I may have a wet with his first lieutenant," Dagan volunteered.

"Aye," Jake said, "and I may get a moment with the master."

"Let's you and me buy a round to give them the opportunity," Gabe said. "You're buying, of course, Coop." This brought smiles to everyone, except Coop.

After a moment, Coop even smiled, "Why not?"

***

IT WAS LATE WHEN everyone returned home, yet lanterns still lit up the house. James, Josie, and their little boy were there, as was Suzanne Bledsoe. They could hear laughter even before they got to the door.

Brand, the stable boy and the blacksmith's helper, ran up. "I'll take care of the horses, Cap'n."

"Thank you, Brand. Why are you still up?"

"Can't nobody sleep wid them wimmins cackling. Mr. James done come out and sat a spell, smoking a cigar to run off these skeeters."

"Let's go rescue James then," Gabe volunteered.

James was not in sight when they walked in. He and Brim had retired to the kitchen. James was filling T in on what crops were money crops, like cotton and tobacco, and then crops like corn for people and livestock.

When the men entered, Faith looked up at her husband and son-in-law. In doing so, she glanced at the wall clock. It was 9:30 p.m., late…too late for James and Josie to head home. Suzanne refused to stay the night, saying that she could be home in twenty minutes. The party broke up and places were found for everyone to sleep.

A candle was lit by Cooper and Maddy's bed. The flame flickered and created shadows on the wall. When Maddy slipped out of her clothes, Cooper could see the shadow of her pregnant belly on the wall. For some reason, he pulled her to where he sat on the bed. He closed his arms around his wife and kissed her belly button.

"I'm getting fat," she said.

"You are beautiful," he replied, meaning it.

"You sail in the morning," Maddy said, a statement and not a question.

"Yes, weather permitting."

"I will pray for thunderstorms then," she said.

Coop had to smile. He stood and finished undressing. As soon as they were lying down, Maddy started kissing him.

"You *are* happy that we are having a child, aren't you, Coop?"

"Yes, darling."

Maddy smiled, "You know that I wanted to give myself to you from the first time we met, Sir Pirate. You could have taken me and I'd have enjoyed every minute."

"I wanted you, but I was married."

"That made me love you more. You believed in keeping your vows."

"I vow to love you as long as I live, Maddy."

"Show me, Coop. Show me how much you wanted me when you saw me lying there naked."

"I'll show you," Coop replied, grabbing a breast.

"Yes, God yes," Maddy whispered. "Harder, Coop."

They made love until they were finally spent. Thunder woke Cooper up at dawn. By daylight, there was a deluge of rain.

"Come back to bed," Maddy said to Coop, who was looking out the window. "I got my wish."

CHAPTER SIXTEEN

TBRIM WAS FOR THE most part a contented man. A good ship beneath him, a moderate breeze filled *Stag's* sails and a mixed crew that seemed to be coming together. The second lieutenant and he had talked about expectations for gunnery and sail handling in private.

Lieutenant James Drury was a bit stiff at first, especially about protocol and discipline, but aside from that their expectations on sailing and fighting the ship mirrored each other. Lieutenant Drury was well liked in the wardroom. He had a good voice and could, on prompt, sing some little verse about any subject brought up. Most of the verses were profane but the other officers enjoyed them immensely.

They had sighted a British merchantman, earlier that day. Sailing within hailing distance, the merchant captain informed them that he'd sighted a ship off Marco Island last evening. The ship had attempted to close with them, but night came on so they darkened the ship and were able to evade what he called the suspicious ship in the night.

Cooper had *Stag's* course changed. His first week aboard the *Raven*, Eli had stopped over at Marco Island where Cooper found several pirate ships with their crews camping out on the small island, which lay just off the southern gulf coast of Florida. The island that came to be known as Key Marco was, at that time, known as Horr's Island, after Captain John Horr. On his first visit to the island, Cooper had thought it was appropriately named as whores were abundant there. It was where he'd first met Talley Brim, T, as the other pirates called him. He was part of Dominique Youx's crew aboard the *Tigre*.

Cooper, T, and Drury met in Cooper's cabin, enjoying a wet as they waited on Brisco, the master, to return with his charts showing Horr's Island. Once Brisco returned, he reluctantly admitted that he had no charts for Key Marco or Horr's Island.

Cooper looked at T and said, "You were Youx's quartermaster. I'm sure that you remember the channel and anchorage well enough."

"I think so, Captain, but I also remember that they had a couple of cannons situated on top of an old Indian burial mound to cover Caxambas Pass. The pass is critical to reaching the island via a ship."

"I think it's best to put a scouting party ashore before we make our presence known," Coop said after discussing the approach to the island.

"Aye, I agree," T said.

Cooper looked at his first officer, "You will stay on board *Stag*, T. Should something happen to me, you are the only one with the pirate savvy to make the operation succeed."

"There's Johannes," T said in protest.

"Aye," Coop agreed, "but he's not here." T shrugged, knowing that further argument was futile.

Cooper had *Swan* signaled to close with *Stag*. He then had Lieutenant Dyea come on board for captain's call and to bring Lieutenant Harvey with him.

Lieutenant James Drury couldn't help but think how a Navy captain would have signaled to *Swan*, 'captain repair on board.' No, Cooper's ways were not the Royal Navy's. But had the Royal Navy's ways worked, he wouldn't be on board this ship now. He'd have been on the beach.

***

HMS *SWAN* CLOSED TO within a mile from shore. It was a cloudy night and so the moon's light was hidden by the clouds. Spurlock, Ox, Banty, and Jimmy Spurlin, the hog hunter and woodsman, were rowed ashore in one of *Swan's* longboats. When the boat ground ashore, the four men jumped out.

Spurlock turned to the midshipman in charge of the boat and said, "Lay off shore about a hundred yards or more. I will signal you with three sparks from my striker. That's your signal to pick us up. Don't return the signal, it might be seen by others."

"Aye, sir," the middy said, and the men shoved the boat off.

Under the cover of darkness, the ex-pirates made their way through the thick mangrove trees until they were on the edge of the pirate encampment.

Spurlock nudged Banty, "I bet that we could walk in and it'd be like old times." Ox and Banty smiled. Spurlock then said, "That's a notion, but we'd better play it straight."

The pirate village was actually larger than Spurlock and his group remembered. Several bonfires lit the place up so that the outline of several ships could be seen.

"Four ships," Banty said. "I guess the island is still remembered by many."

"Aye," the group replied.

Laughter could be heard coming out of the nearest hut. A woman ran out with her naked breasts visible.

"What catheads," Ox groaned. "Sure brings back old memories." They all smiled again.

Another woman cried out. She was being pulled along by some rogue. As they reached the shack, the man said something to the topless wench. She slapped the other girl on the face and shouted at her. The woman bent over to pick up a jug and the wench kicked her in the arse, knocking her down.

"Captive," Spurlock said. "They have captive women."

"Aye, at least one," Banty agreed.

With the fires blazing, a large number of men could be made out. "There are three hundred men here," Spurlock said. "Four crews at least."

"There sure is. We'll have our work cut out for us," Ox said.

"We'll have surprise on our side," Spurlin said.

"I hope so," Ox said, looking back

***

SPURLOCK LAID OUT THEIR findings back on board *Stag*.

"Better than we hoped for," *Swan's* Captain Dyea volunteered.

"I'm not so sure," Cooper said. "Three hundred pirates, each a fighting man, each knowing to be captured means the gallows."

"Do we wait for reinforcements?" Lieutenant Drury asked.

"No...no," Cooper replied. "We'll attack...at dawn."

Swan landed the marines from both ships with Banty and Ox as their guides. Spurlock and Spurlin each headed up a party of seamen. The marines were to come in from the rear, cutting off escape while the sailors would hit the pirates on the flank. Spurlin's job was to cut down anyone attempting to do harm to the captives. He carried three rifles and had two men to keep his guns loaded for him.

According to Spurlock and his group of men who had scouted the island, the pirates must have made a good haul. They had put on a feast, roasting boars over fire pits. There were kegs of rum scattered about, as were jugs of various spirits. Women captives had been used and abused. Cooper knew that to give them their freedom they had to plan the assault and not just attack with cannons roaring. The prisoners would have surely died then. Cooper looked at his timepiece for about the third or fourth time in the last ten minutes.

"Not long now, Captain," came from T.

Overhead the clouds had moved out and the moon shone down bright in the predawn. Looking once more at his watch, Cooper gave the word to set sail. The wind caused the sails to billow a time or two before they filled with a snap. Drury had the watch. He, better than anyone, knew the ship.

Cooper looked aft and *Swan* was gliding along just off to larboard. His mind went to the cannons. Were they still there? Had they been manned? If so, were they manned by a crew who took their jobs seriously or were they sleeping off a drunk like their comrades?

"The pass is dead ahead," Cooper heard Brisco, the master, telling Lieutenant Drury.

Up ahead, the gunners were at their guns. They were to hold the pirate ships at anchor to keep them from getting underway. T had joked, 'I doubt that out of the four ships there aren't enough sober men to be found to crew one ship.'

In silence, under a full moon, the two ships sailed into position. Cooper Cain had now evolved from pirate to pirate hunter. A job that he felt may erase his actions from the past.

"There are the ships, Coop," Dagan said, bringing his friend's mind back to the job at hand.

Cooper raised his hand. When he brought it down they'd put the helm down so that *Stag* could pass down the line of ships, giving the gun captains sitting targets. *Swan* would train her swivels on the rogues ashore. As soon as the swivels were fired, the sailors ashore would attack. *Swan* would, given time, come about for another pass. It remained to be seen if there was room for *Stag* to come about or if she would anchor and fire at targets of opportunity.

Cooper watched and waited just a few more seconds. He then yelled and the ship's wheel spun. The deck canted as *Stag* turned. As soon as *Stag* righted itself the cannons roared. The deck planking vibrated as each gun spewed forth its lethal mass of ball and grape. The gunners worked with a fury, not wanting to be last reloading.

BOOM...BOOM. The stillness of the dawn was broken by the thunder of each gun, closely followed by its neighbor. Ashore the smaller bang of musket and pistol fire was heard. The beach was in chaos. Pirates woke up to the sound of cannon fire. It seemed each way they turned they were met with deadly fire. Screams, curses, and cries for help all blended together.

Jimmy Spurlin kept his rifles firing, as first one rogue and then another tried to use a captive for a shield. Men were soon running toward the mangrove swamp. Some were shot down by the marines, but more than a few managed to make it. Some of the men were wounded and limping, while others were running all out. One of the captive women picked up a pistol from a dead pirate and shot the man who had dragged her into his hut the night before.

The battle was soon over. The pirates laid down their arms and surrendered. *Stag* was anchored with her guns trained on shore. Cooper and T went ashore to get things organized. The first person Cooper saw was the first mate off one of the company's ships.

"Thank God, somebody has come to our rescue."

"I'm glad that we came in time, Martin," Cooper said.

"It was Hague," Martin shouted. "He sailed up to our ship like mates passing and then he took us."

Robert Hague had been a privateer out of Charlestown. He held up his hand, "I give up, Coop. There's no fight left in me."

"Why, Robert?" Coop asked. "Why did you turn?"

"My last captures were after the war was over, Coop. I didn't come away with anything but debt."

Cooper shook his head. "I would have helped, Robert."

"Aye, I know you would have, Coop. But what's done is done."

"You know what they'll do to you at home, Robert."

"Yes, I know. We all know, Coop. If it's just the same with you, we'd just as soon have it done with here. There's family at home, Coop. I would not want to put them through the embarrassment."

Cooper nodded, "Robert, who is Calico?"

Hague stared at his former friend a moment. "I can't say as I rightly know, Coop. I only had a glimpse of him once. His lieutenant was the one who gave us our area to patrol. We were actually waiting on him here."

"When were you supposed to meet with this lieutenant?" Coop asked.

"That's just it, Coop, you never know. A day, a week. Once it was two months. They figure if you don't know you can't tell."

"I'm sure that goes well with your crew," Coop replied.

"Why not," Hague said. "They got all they want here."

Dagan walked up. He'd been with Diamond searching the different ships. They'd come up with a lot of loot but no letters or correspondence of any sort that would prove useful.

Cooper turned to Hague, "You've one hour to make your peace, Robert."

Hague nodded and then turned a barrel over and sat on it. Dagan questioned the other captains while Cooper talked to his men and Captain Dyea.

"There are nearly a hundred captives here," Spurlock volunteered. "That surely limits the room on our ships, doesn't it?"

"Aye," the group replied.

"Are there any ideas where most of them are from?" Coop asked.

"Some of them sound British, Cap'n. Of course, not all of them are, though. A few of them have pointed out some of the rogues who murdered people. Some of them were murdered after being on the island."

"Find out who they are and line them up."

"Aye, Cap'n."

"We don't have room to transport the pirates and the captives," Coop said. "I intend to hang the four captains and shoot the murderers. We'll empty out the ships and burn them. The rest of the pirates will have to make do with what's left."

A firing squad was made up of marines; those pirates who had committed murder and rape were shot. The four pirate ships were set ablaze.

When Cooper approached the captains, he asked if there was anyone to notify. None replied. "Any last words?"

Hague spoke then. "Thank you, Cooper, for sparing our families."

"I hate this, Robert."

Hague smiled and said, "Not as much as I do." The man then reached, out touching Cooper's shoulder. "Be careful with Calico, Coop. He isn't human. He even looks like a demon and that's from a distance."

The men were then hanged. It had been a complete victory, but Cooper felt down. The hanging of a former friend didn't sit well.

* * *

JOHANNES AND LIEUTENANT LUDLOW of *Swallow* were at the rendezvous when *Stag* and *Swan* arrived. They had not seen a single ship that wasn't what they appeared to be. Cooper told them of their find and to wait for Captain Lanning of *Syren*. They were then to patrol the Virgin Islands while he took the people that they'd rescued to Antigua.

"How long do I wait?" Johannes asked.

"Just as we set it," Coop said. He had a sudden premonition that Captain Lanning wouldn't show up.

CHAPTER SEVENTEEN

RAIN SLANTED ALMOST HORIZONTALLY out of the west. It was driven by a wind that bent the tall palm trees and made a noise that varied between a roar and a whistling sound. Overhead, black clouds scudded along. At times, they almost obscured the tall main mast on *Minotaur*, Admiral Davy's flagship.

A solitary soul braved the wind and rain as he passed T Brim on horseback. The man was hunched over so much that T hoped the horse knew where it was going, as the man's head was bent so low that he couldn't see a thing in front of him. T had come ashore in Cooper's gig. The rain had hit just as the gig came alongside of the flagship. The boat crew then took T ashore and were hopefully back at *Stag* by now.

Shirreffs, the young gentleman in charge of the boat, was lucky Quang was with him. It was Quang, Cooper's Chinese cox'n, who pushed the boy down in the boat and then shoved off from the shore. The young gentleman's eyes had been wild with fear and his teeth were chattering from the cold hard rain.

Lieutenant Drury felt that having the young gentleman in the boat was called for in keeping with Navy protocol. T wasn't sure it was worth it, but there were a lot of things strange to him about the Navy. However, hunting pirates was not the usual thing that the Navy did. At least, someone with a brain was convinced that it took somebody like Cooper Cain to head up the operation.

A sudden gust of wind almost pushed T over. His slicker had had a small rip in it. Now, the wind had torn it so that the tattered slicker flapped wildly and noisily. Water cascaded from his hat brim. Were he not almost to his destination, he would have found a shelter and hopefully a full tankard of rum. Stepping up the steps and under the stoop T knocked on the door. He hadn't seen a carriage or horse in the stable as he avoided the main entrance to Cooper's mother's home. The service entrance was the one Dolcie would use. T knocked louder, thinking that weather had or could have caused his first knock to be unheard.

Dolcie would be surprised …if she was even at home. On a day such as this, though, where else would she be. T was about to knock again when the door opened a crack.

"Yes," Dolcie inquired.

"It's me, Dolcie," T said, taking his hat off.

Dolcie flung the door open and taking his arm pulled him in. She circled her arms around T, embracing him and kissing him warmly and passionately.

"Dolcie, you'll be soaked."

"I don't care. You don't know how I've longed for you." She took the tattered slicker and threw it out the door. She then started undressing T. Sitting on a three legged stool, T got his wet boots off.

A small fire had been lit in the fireplace to combat the dampness and the chill. Dolcie pulled three chairs over and hung T's clothes over the chair backs so that the fire would dry them. The boots were placed alongside but not too close. Otherwise, the leather would shrink.

With T standing naked, Dolcie came to him again. She gave him a quick kiss and took his hand. "Come with me to my chamber, sir. I think that I may be able to warm you up and get rid of the chill."

T smiled, "I was hoping you might."

He sat on the edge of the bed as Dolcie slowly and deliberately undressed. "I've missed you," he said.

"I can see," Dolcie said softly.

***

COOPER WAS WARMLY RECEIVED by Captain Jake Anthony and Admiral Davy. He had been surprised when the flagship's challenge had come down and the midshipman replied *Stag*. When his head came level with the entry port, pipes had sounded as he was piped on board. Even in a downpour the Navy stood on tradition. Jake had shook his hand and said, "The admiral is waiting."

Cooper quickly told them about the tip they'd gotten from the merchant captain. He told about sending out a scouting party and upon their return, the raid. He continued with the telling of putting those known to have committed murder, rape, and torture before a firing squad. He also told of hanging the four pirate captains.

"If there hadn't been so many captives, I may have brought the captains back for trial." What he did not say was that Robert Hague, once a fellow privateer, had asked to have the sentence carried out at once to avoid embarrassment to his family. The number of captives seemed reason enough to do so.

"I will say, Admiral, that Lieutenant Drury, being a gentleman, protested my leaving the pirates that we hanged dangling on a rope. I told him it was to send a message."

"Any better idea on who this Captain Calico is?" Jake asked.

"No! I...actually knew one of the pirates, Captain. We were, at one time, friends of a sort. Before he was hanged, he told me to be careful in dealing with Calico. He said, one – that he wasn't human and two – he was a devil."

"It sounds like he knew the man," Admiral Davy responded.

"No…no he didn't. He never was even close to the man and had, in fact, only seen him from a distance. Calico has a lieutenant, a henchman of sorts that relays all of his orders. He does seem to be well organized. He assigns his pirates certain areas to carry out their deeds and then sends a henchman to certain locations to collect the loot and captives."

"I see," Admiral Davy said. "When the weather moderates, Coop, we'll send boats to take off your guests. I'm sure Governor Basnight will want to hear all that you've told me, so expect an invitation. Take a few days and visit your mother while I see that your ships are replenished. I'm sure with so many mouths to feed that your supplies are low."

"Thank you, Admiral," Coop responded.

Jake then asked, "How are the naval officers doing?"

Coop paused to gather his thoughts, "Lieutenant Drury and my man, Brim, have become friends. I think each one of them is learning things that will serve them for years to come. *Swan's* Captain Dyea is a good man. He's eager, wants to please, and asks a question when something isn't clear. I have every faith in him. I do see Lieutenant Drury looking at *Swan* at times. The first prize that I take will be sent back with him in command. Captain Lanning is a sullen man. I'm not sure he likes his assignment. He did not show up at the rendezvous when I expected him to be the first one there. I sent him into the Gulf of Mexico as an escort but also to observe and report back anything he felt was suspicious."

Admiral Davy had his pipe in his hands and twirled it around. "I did not know the captain prior to his assignment to this squadron, so other than having proven he's a capable man, I can't tell you anything about him. I do agree that he's acted like something isn't right with him. It's as you say, sullen. If I need to replace him, let me know."

"Let's give him a chance first," Coop said.

Jake then asked, "Is Dagan with you?"

"Aye, he told me that he'd see you later. He didn't feel like getting out in the weather. This is before the rain set in, mind you." Jake and the admiral both laughed.

"I will make sure if Dagan calls, that he'll be piped on board," Jake said, bringing smiles from the admiral and Cooper.

When Cooper was leaving, the admiral called to him. "Coop, I like the idea of putting Drury in a prize. That will go a long way toward helping him get his step up."

Coop smiled, "Consider it done, Admiral."

CHAPTER EIGHTEEN

THE SUN SEEMED TO emerge suddenly on the horizon. It appeared out of the distant edge of the sea, like a man who had just awakened and, once he was awake, rose up quickly. Cooper stood, looking out the stern window, in his cabin. He closed his eyes and savored the easterly breeze. The breeze, even in his cabin, was enough to tousle his hair and cause his open cotton shirt to puff out and flutter.

The ship was quiet except for the sounds made by any ship at sea. Cooper, from his point at the most distant part of the ship, could make out the splash against the bow as the ship rhythmically rose up and then plunged down through another wave. There was the sound of water rushing down the scuppers and the occasional groan from the mast. He could not believe the difference in the ship after getting all of the captive women off. A constant cacophony of women's voices would not be missed.

Cooper, gazing out over the swells and occasional white caps, found himself thinking of one woman captive, in particular. She was young, but having seen the pirates murder her husband, and she, herself having been raped several times, had become hardened. Her face was broad and her cheekbones high, with a wide mouth and full lips. But there was no softness in her expression. She had tied her long black hair at the nape of her neck. She would be a prize catch for most men, she had, in fact, been. That was before the pirates. She'd approached Cooper wearing a thin cotton shirt that she'd gotten from a sailor. The shirt showed the deep V between her full breasts. If she was aware...or cared that the brown of her nipples were visible, she didn't show it.

"You don't have a doctor on board this ship, Captain?" Her statement was a matter-of-fact. "My husband was a surgeon. I've assisted him more than a few times, doing all kinds of surgeries. He once said that I was a better surgeon than he was."

Cooper listened but didn't say a word. Dagan stood to the side, with an amused look on his face.

"You need a surgeon," she said. "I want to kill pirates. I think that we would be a good match."

A long pause passed before either of them spoke. Finally, it was Dagan who spoke. "There are women on board a lot of ships in various roles, including surgeon's mates. Therefore, having you on board would not be a novel idea. You must understand, though, that you are younger and more beautiful than most. You could sleep in the sick bay, which has its own head, and dine in the wardroom as most surgeons do."

"So you will take me, Captain?" she asked.

Cooper thought for a moment. He had seen this woman shoot one blackheart with a pistol and run another through with a sword. She was tough alright...hardened and tough. "I've heard other women call you Kate," he said. "Is that your name? I'll need it to enter you on the ship's roll." For the first time, Cooper saw Kate's face soften and she smiled.

"Kathryn...Kathryn Timberlake, but for most I've always been just Kate," she said.

Cooper held out his hand to shake Kate's. "One thing, Kate, we will sail in two days. You will need to go ashore and buy what surgical and medical supplies that you think we need. My man, Josiah, will assist you."

"Thank you, Captain," Kate responded. "You won't be sorry."

Cooper smiled and glanced down at her shirt once more and felt a stirring in him. "One more thing, Kate, buy yourself some clothes. The…ah…the ones you have on now can be very distracting."

Kate looked down at her shirt and smiled. Turning to go, she paused and looked back at Coop. She smiled again and winked as she left.

Dagan smiled and said, "I think that's one who can handle a man, Coop. Be it cutlass, pistol, or wiles."

"I agree," Cooper said. "We'll keep this meeting to ourselves. Maddy would be furious."

"Aye, that she would be," Dagan replied. "But Coop, I can see that they are much alike."

***

WILLIAM HOUSE, ONCE A Royal marine who now acted as Cooper's secretary and Josiah's assistant, found himself staring at Kate. He had helped carry the medical supplies down to sick bay the day before they sailed. He had entered her in the ship's muster book and now needed her signature. Waiting on Kate to stow away her supplies, House found himself thinking what it would be like having such a woman as his wife. He was still daydreaming when Kate touched his arm.

"Are you with the living?" she asked.

"I'm sorry, my mind was far away," he replied.

Kate smiled and took the log. The page was earmarked so she turned to it, signed and gave the log back to House. As he left, he passed Dagan in the passageway. *He's in love*, Dagan thought with a smile. *He may be the first but he wouldn't be the last*. If Dagan would admit it, even he found the woman waking up desires that had not stirred since his wife, Betsy, had died. The sound of the lookout calling down 'sails to larboard' broke Dagan's reverie. *Damme*, he thought. *Does she have me moonstruck like some young midshipman?*

On deck, it wasn't long before the lookout called down, "It's *SeaFire*, and *Swallow*, Cap'n."

Cooper looked over at T and Drury. "*SeaFire* and *Swallow*, but no *Syren*."

Where had Captain Lanning gone? Was he in trouble? Had he run into a bad squall? Had he been taken? So damn many ifs.

Once the ships came up together, Cooper had a captain's call. Neither Captain Ludlow from *Swallow* or Captain Dyea from *Swan* could come up with some insight to explain Lanning's missing.

"He was a loner," Dyea said, "but he followed orders. I think for him to not make rendezvous twice means that something has happened."

"He was sent to the gulf, so let's search in that direction," Coop said.

"Aye," Johannes agreed. "We've not seen anything in our area. Maybe we'll find something there."

The squadron sailed for three days towards Mobile. It was on the third day that they came upon a fishing yawl.

"Have *Swallow* heave to and talk with the old man who owns the boat," Coop ordered.

He then signaled *SeaFire* and *Swan*. When *Stag* was up on *Swallow* and the fishing boat, Ludlow boarded *Stag*, and had the fisherman with him.

"This is John James, Captain. He and his sons fish this area routinely. Last week a ship about the size of *Stag* stopped him and gave him a note. It was addressed to Cooper Cain. Apparently, they left copies of the note with fishermen all along the coast, above and below Mobile."

Cooper opened the note and read, 'You will find your captain from whence you came. I now have your ship. — Calico'

"Hell's fire," Cooper swore. "Did you read this?"

"Aye, Captain."

Cooper turned to the fisherman. "Thank you, sir. You have my gratitude." He then gave the old man twenty dollars as he saw him over the side.

"Where to, Captain?" T asked.

"From whence we came," Cooper said, repeating what he'd read in the note.

T looked at Cooper for a minute and then turned to the master. "Come about, Mister Brisco, and set a course for Key Marco."

"Aye, Mr. Brim."

Bosun pipes broke the stillness and feet padded on the deck as *Stag's* crew went to their stations.

Cooper thought, *how did Calico know his name? Obviously from Lanning, but what else did he know?*

***

IT WAS MID MORNING of the second day that they reached Marco Island. Cooper had the ships anchor in deep water and went ashore with a party of men in a longboat. The stench hit them as the boats ground into the sandy beach. Captain Lanning was hung spread eagle-like from two trees. His officers were hung by the neck from nearby trees. Lieutenant Lewis Potts moved to cut Lanning down.

"Stop," Spurlin shouted. He had the men step back and shot the lower rope tied to the tree. The rope parted with one shot and as it let go, an arm swung up out of the ground with stakes drove in it. Had a man cut the rope, he would have been impaled.

"How did you know?" Lieutenant Potts asked.

Spurlin responded, "I didn't see the end of the rope. It made me wonder what it was attached to."

"Thank you," Potts said. "I would have died a horrible death, surely."

CHAPTER NINETEEN

R OUNDING THE FLORIDA KEYS, a group of merchant ships was
spotted. It was not really a convoy as such, but the ships
sailed together to offer some protection to each other. Cooper
was not surprised to see the Savannah Import/Export flag
flying from two of the ships. When they got up to the merchant
men, Cooper saw the *Mary Esther*. She was Buck Jewell's ship
and named after his bride. The two ships sailed within hailing
distance.

Buck, after the pleasantries were over, related how two ships
closed on them just before dark last evening. He and the other
company ship opened their gun ports and rolled out their cannons, presenting ten guns between the two of them. The two
ships then went about and headed in an east-southeasterly
direction.

"Toward the Bahamas," T volunteered.

After saying farewell and asking Buck to call on Maddy,
Cooper had the ships come about and set a course for the
Bahamas.

"We'll call on Nassau first," Cooper said to T and Drury. "It
was once a beehive of pirate activity, maybe there are some still
about."

Nassau had grown considerably since T had last set foot
ashore. Several of the old *Raven's* crew broke up into groups and
combed the streets trying to find out any possible information. T
fell in with Johannes Ewers, Banty, and Ox.

At one hole in the wall tavern occupied by a seedier group of sailors, a voice called out, "T, by gawd it's T." A wizened old pirate, who had lost a leg, limped over. "It appears that you've done well, T. Me lucks not been so good."

Fishing a coin from his purse, T greeted the old sailor. "Ethan… Ethan Adams. It's been a while."

The old sailor beamed, pleased at being recognized. "Has ye got room for an extra hand…as a cook maybe?"

"I'm not the captain or quartermaster anymore," T replied. "I might have a way that ye can earn a few extra coins, though."

Ethan straightened himself up, trying to hold himself erect, instead of leaning over on his crutch. "What manner o' service is it that you need?"

T leaned over and whispered in the old sailor's ear, "We are searching for Calico."

The old man pushed back so fast, he would have fallen had Ox not grabbed him. "You can get yer throat slit just by mentioning that name, T. Gawd man, you don't plan to join up with Satan, do you?" Ethan's reaction let the men know that the old man knew of Calico.

"No, let's just say that I have a score to settle with the man," T responded.

"Forget ye score. He has spies everywhere. I was told that he never sleeps in the same place twice. He's not one to truck with, T. He don't just kill a man, he mutilates them. He often lets his boys do it and if they don't, he does it for them."

"Boys," T repeated.

"Aye, I hear that he prefers the Windward Passage, be it a boy or young girl."

"You have no idea where he has his base of operation?" T asked

"No, but if I did, I'd only tell if I was taken away from here," Ethan replied.

T looked around the small room. "I'll check back with you, Ethan. If you have something I'll get you away from here."

"Come back tomorrow, T. I might be able to help you then." T flipped the old man another coin as they got ready to leave.

Johannes noticed the man behind the bar was staring, so he spoke out, "If we can get you on as the cook's helper, we'll come back." Johannes was not sure that this little ruse would fool anyone, but he was glad to see the old sailor lift his hand in acknowledgment.

Later that evening, the crews reported that they had come up with little information. Spurlock and Diamond had heard one sailor telling another that it was de Corsia who decided whether or not a man was taken to the boss. It was the boss who said yes…or no. If it was no, you were never heard from again.

***

COOPER CAIN SAT ACROSS from Dagan with Captains Dyea and Ludlow to either side. They were seated in one of the finer inns on the island, enjoying a tasty serving of beef with a better than average wine. Several well dressed patrons came and went, a few commenting on seeing British Navy uniforms on Nassau. Towards the end of the meal, however, a man at a table of four grew loud. The owner tried to intervene but one look from the loud mouth sent him back behind the counter. While the loud mouth made a show of being nearly drunk and sloshing red wine on the linen, he didn't fool Dagan or Cooper. Finally, loud mouth rose up, knocking his chair over.

It slammed to the floor with a loud bang, causing everyone in the inn to turn their heads toward the table.

"It's bad enough that we have these stinking Britishers here, but they've some lickspittle up their arse."

No doubt, loud mouth expected Cooper to rise, so he was shocked to see the older Dagan rise up from his chair. The surprise was so complete that loud mouth closed his mouth, not knowing how to proceed.

Dagan, as was his wont, was soft spoken, his voice little more than a whisper. "I, sir, find the use of the word Britisher totally offensive. Even more so since the island is a British colony with the governor, Charles Cameron, residing atop Mount Fitzwilliam. However, I assume your ignorance arrives from the fact that you are French. You are French, are you not, sir?"

Dagan had heard the waiter call the man LeRoux. Loud mouth obviously didn't recall that as he stood quietly, his mouth agape.

"I have in my day killed numerous Frenchmen," Dagan continued. "Some died at the thought of my coming for them, but that was some time ago…and I didn't want to ruin a good meal and superb wine with the death of another Frenchman, ignorant though he may be." Dagan paused, and he seemed to look directly at loud mouth and then took a step back. "Egad man, what's that in your hair? Is it a bat? Close your mouth, man, before the bat gets in it and you swallow the creature."

LeRoux swatted at his head.

Dagan stepped back and ducked. "Don't swat it at me. My sakes, man, there's two bats. Don't let them bite you."

LeRoux was swatting and weaving about, cursing and crying to his companions to help him. He constantly turned his head swatting the air. "Help me," he yelled and started running. His friends took off after him.

Ludlow, Dyea, and Cooper continued to sit and watch, with not a word passed between them. Outside, the cries and curses continued into the distance. A gunshot was then heard.

"I fear LeRoux has killed himself trying to get the bats out of his hair. It's a funny thing how one's mind will play tricks on itself with the slightest provocation."

"There were no bats," Ludlow said, almost like a question.

"None that I saw," Dagan responded, "but something told me that the man had a fear of bats. He also seemed to fear the stories of vampire bats. These were first discovered in the 15th and 16th centuries. Vampires or blood sucking people became folklore."

Cooper smiled, "What was the something, Dagan? I confess I missed it."

Dagan smiled, "First he smelled of garlic and then when he turned, I saw a string with cloves of garlic around his neck."

"I don't understand," Ludlow said.

Dagan replied, "For centuries, stories have been told of vampires. People who have died but are undead. They feast on the blood of live people, killing them, but they turn into vampires.

Bats, especially a certain type of bat, are associated with vampires. People who believe in vampires wear apotropaics. These are items to ward off vampires. Aside from a crucifix or holy water, the most common thing to ward off vampires is garlic." The men all laughed.

"What if he hadn't fallen for your ruse?" Dyea asked.

Dagan looked very stern as he spoke, "I would have had to kill him, then."

***

THE NEXT DAY T, with Ox and Spurlin, went back to the tavern looking for Ethan. The man behind the bar told them that he'd gone out back. The group saw their man leaning over some crates. They noticed a dark stain on the crate as they got near it. T lifted Ethan up. His throat had been slit.

"Oh, Ethan," T groaned. The dead man's hand was still clutching his crutch.

"Look," Ox said.

Ethan had something in his hand besides the shaft of the crutch. Spurlin pried the man's hand open and a paper fell out. One word was written on the paper...'Andros'.

CHAPTER TWENTY

COOPER SAT WITH HIS captains around the table in his cabin. 'Andros'...was Ethan referring to Andros Island in the Bahamas? A man named Andros or maybe some other place?

Brisco brought in his charts of the Bahamas when summoned. "Andros Island has a large reef. The chart doesn't show any channel through it, but I believe there has to be one. Henry Morgan, the pirate, is said to have used the island and hidden much of his booty in a cave beneath a bluff."

"How far is it from Andros to, say, Nassau?"

"Roughly sixty miles," Brisco replied, after using his calipers.

"Less than a day's sail, depending on conditions," Cooper said.

"If Morgan used it, I see no reason that Calico wouldn't," T volunteered.

"Yes," Brisco responded.

"But Andros is a big island. Last I heard, it was sparsely populated, other than loyalists that left the Colonies during the First Revolutionary War." This came from T, who probably had done more than a little pirating in the area with Dominique Youx.

"Were the loyalists receptive to you?" Cooper asked.

"Aye, off the course as they were, we always had things that they desired. But what I'd consider most important," T said, "was that they had a few taverns and a handful of wenches, mostly mulattos. They would not have the number of wenches, though, that it would take to entertain the men sailing for Calico."

"So you think Andros is not the island that we are looking for?" Cooper asked.

"I think it's worth a look, but I don't think its Calico's stronghold," T responded.

"Maybe we'll find a clue," Captain Dyea offered.

"Let's hope so," Coop replied.

The small squadron picked its way through the channel that led to the island. There was a large barrier reef that some called the 'Tongue of the Ocean.' Approaching the anchorage, they saw a coastal trader was anchored, and off to the larboard a pair of fishing boats. Gulls hovered over the boats as two men pulled on a net on the closest boat. A sand bar was visible off to starboard.

Kate walked over to T. "They're beautiful, aren't they?" she said, pointing to a flock of pink and white spoonbills.

"Aye," T responded. "At first, I thought that they were flamingos, like the ones on the beach."

"They aren't as tall," Kate said.

Near the quarterdeck, Lieutenant Drury called to Coop. "On the trader, Captain."

Cooper had already spied the man, probably the captain waving at them. "We'll pay the man a visit once we've anchored, I think."

Lieutenant Drury went about his duties of anchoring the ship, while Cooper went to his cabin and put on something a bit more presentable. Josiah was waiting with the freshly brushed captain's coat and hat.

"Sword?" Quang asked. Cooper nodded and his cox'n buckled it around Cooper's waist.

Damned if they aren't getting to be like regular Navy, Coop thought.

Dagan came in and said, "I hear the island has a blue hole that a monster fish-like creature lives in. It's said to be half dragon and half octopus. Wrecked boats and vanishing swimmers are said to be from this Lusca." Cooper smiled as Dagan spoke of the Lusca. "I was thinking," Dagan continued, "if we find Calico here, why not feed him to the Lusca."

Cooper, Josiah, and Quang all laughed. "That's damnable cruel," Cooper said.

Dagan looked sternly at Coop, "To who? The Lusca or Calico." Now, they all laughed again.

Once he could stop laughing, Coop told Quang to have the midshipman on watch get his boat ready to go ashore. "Quang, tell T that I'd like for him to accompany me." Quang gave a quick nod and left.

"You are welcome to come as well," Cooper said, speaking to Dagan. Then as an afterthought, he spoke again, "I assume you knew that."

"Aye, Coop. I think that I'll see if Kate would like to come ashore with me."

Coop wondered as Dagan left, if old Dagan had romantic desires toward Kate. But then Coop thought, *Dagan likes the woman. He knows what she has gone through. He is trying to be a friend, maybe a fatherly like relationship.* He doubted that it was romantic. That was a different story, though…with most of the other men. He had even noticed T looking at Kate.

The wind had been blowing and her blouse looked like it was pasted to her body, her wares were very prominent. T had seen her and looked away, and then his gaze immediately swept back. *Hell,* Coop thought, *I found myself looking as well, not a man alive could have helped looking.*

✳✳✳

Captain Dean Ledford shook Cooper's hand and introduced himself. They were invited to walk up the beach to Ledford's house and enjoy some cool refreshments. Cooper explained why the squadron had sailed to the island as they walked up to the house.

"Well, sir, there are no pirates here, nor much of anything else. The pirate, Morgan, was said to have used the island and maybe others; but nothing recently. I have had a scare or two from the rascals, however. Were my vessel not made for shallow waters, I'm afraid we'd have been taken. My neighbor had more than a scare. His boat was holed by what he thought was a Royal Navy frigate. Luckily, he was able to make it to a cay and avoided capture."

Cooper gave T a knowing look. "One of our frigates was on escort duty," Cooper said. "We received word that she had been taken and where to find her crew. They had all been killed."

"That's hellish of the blackhearts," Ledford responded. "Why don't you and your captains come for supper tonight? Trevor should be back and you can talk to him about his experience. In the meantime, we have ample fresh water, if you need to replenish your stores. I might say, Captain, the reason that I've stayed on the island when a good many loyalists gave up, is the water supply. We still farm, but for produce. We grow cucumbers, lettuce, and we also have a few citrus trees that grow grapefruits and limes. We also have a few acres of bananas, pineapple, and mangoes. We have found that cattle do fairly well and our chickens give plenty of eggs. We've several acres of sugar cane, of course. We could sell a few chickens or cows if you need them."

"I will notify our captains," Cooper said, "and thank you for your dinner invitation. We'll be glad to accept."

Kate spoke then, "I've read where the islands have many natural medicines. Could you tell me about them?"

Ledford replied, "Our woman, Carrie, can tell you all about those. She was a slave child when we left Carolina. My wife said that when we arrived on Andros we were starting a new life and she would not do it with slaves, so we freed all of them. Carrie's mother was my wife's servant. When my wife died, Carrie, who'd taken over her mother's duties, just took over the house. I love her to death. When I'm gone, this will all be hers." Ledford excused himself then to go get Carrie.

Dagan said, when he'd gone, "If you look out that window, you can see four graves, likely his wife and children."

Ledford quickly returned with a short woman who had a big smile. "You look for medicines," she said. "We got a few here. There's the bay geranium. You boil it in a tea with lime and salt. It cures you when your body aches and you got green or yellow coming out of your nose or you cough it up. For burns, from the sun or fire, you peel the bark from the red peeling gumbo-limbo trees."

Carrie then said, smiling even bigger, "We got the love vine on this island. People say it makes great loves for them that eat the leaves when fixed right. Mr. Ledford says he too old for a woman. I told him if he brings a white woman home, I'll fix him a love potion and she will never leave."

"Hush, Carrie," Ledford said in mock anger, but everyone was laughing.

"Maybe we'll get some for Dagan," Kate said, with a smile. This brought the laughter back.

Dagan smiled and responded, "What makes you think that I need a potion?"

CHAPTER TWENTY ONE

THE MEAL AT MR. Ledford's house was a big success. Chickens must have been plentiful, as Carrie and her kitchen help delivered up a dinner that reminded Coop of Rosa and home.

"I assumed that you sailors probably have more fish in your diet than desired. I thought a poultry feast was in order."

Neither the captains nor their lieutenants were brash enough to tell the planter that sailors seldom eat fish.

Cooper met Trevor. There was no other name given, so Cooper didn't ask. Trevor had a coastal trader much like Ledford. He then told Cooper of the incident that Ledford had spoken of.

"He had been in the area of Crooked Island and Acklins. He did some trading or had been doing some trading there. This big frigate seemed to come out of nowhere. At first, I thought her a British warship. Then I saw the slovenly way she was sailed and I knew better. We had the wind advantage and it was dusk. We ducked into a small cay, still we were holed. A ball narrowly missed the rudder. When it got dark they sailed away. We worked hard to plug the hole with planks torn from my cabin. With the planks and a piece of sail, we fothered the hole and, using the pumps, we made it back home."

"What's there to attract a bunch of cutthroats?" T asked.

"There's a fresh water well that was dug, a long time back, by French pirates. There's an abandoned British fort there as well. I imagine the cutthroats have taken control of it. It lies at what's called Gun Point."

"Would it be hard to land a party on the island to get an idea about the best way to take the fort?"

Trevor smiled. "Ain't nobody yet been able to do it. First the pirates, and then the British set up on the area, and nobody ever pried them out. The fort and French well is sheltered by the cays between Long Cay and Crooked Island on one side, and by the shallow flats known as 'The Bight of Acklins.' This is the area where the French pirates used to hide their ships. When merchant ships using the Crooked Island Passage came by, the pirates would board their hidden ships and sail out and attack them. That's why the British built the fort there, to keep out privateers during the war. Now that these cutthroats have it, I'll guarantee the British wish that they'd never left it."

Cooper made a note to talk with Brisco, *Stag's* master. He wanted a look at the charts. Trevor painted a frightful picture of the situation. *If need be*, Coop thought, *he'd keep the ships pinned up in the passage and send word to Admiral Davy*. There was little doubt that *Minotaur* could smash the fort with her big guns. But hopefully, he'd find a way to take the island.

***

THE MEAL WAS OVER and the men gathered out on a covered patio. Ledford passed out Cuban cigars and brought out a bottle of amber colored spirits. "My dear fellows, this is the last bottle of Old Jake Beam Sour Mash, or as some call it now…bourbon. I've been waiting on a special occasion to pop the cork. Sharing it with such stout fellows as you is occasion enough."

A black youth, who looked to be about twelve years of age, started handing out cigars and small glasses. When he got to Lieutenant Drury, the good lieutenant waved the boy off.

"I'm afraid good Cuban cigars and fine bourbon would be a waste on me," Drury said.

T looked up in disbelief, his jaw hanging down. "What's that, James, you turning down the best of cigars and alcohol?"

Drury responded, "I fear they'd be wasted on me as I'm no connoisseur of the better spirits or tobacco."

T shook his head in disgust. He then had everyone laughing at his reply, "Damme, James, even a dog knows the difference in a steak bone and a chicken bone."

After the laughter ended, Lieutenant James Drury, Royal Navy, smoked his first Cuban cigar and tasted his first American made bourbon.

***

GORDON BRISCO SET HIS charts down on Cooper's table. The captains of the other ships looked down at the charts. The stern windows and the skylight were all open to let in more light and hopefully a bit of a breeze.

"Crooked Island opens into the Windward Passage, the dividing point between the Caribbean and the Bahamas," Brisco explained.

A note fixed to the chart said the island was once called Fragrant Island. The chart pointed out two places, Pittstown Point with a landing deep enough for a large boat but no real soundings. Near the settlement was a note that said British Fort. Someone had made a note that read, 'cave near Gun Bluff.' The other notation was Colonel Hill.

"When was this chart made?" Coop asked.

Brisco answered with a rare smile, "1789 or there about. It means that someone took an older chart and added to it, the additions of the fort, more-than-likely. Obviously there is nothing about a channel. I wonder why."

"There were not good landings. He probably meant that wasn't visible from the fort or Colonel Hill," T volunteered.

"Maybe," Dyea agreed.

A cry, from overhead, was heard, "Sumthin in the water, just off the larboard bow."

"I'll go up," T said.

Midshipman Shirreffs was soon at the door. "First lieutenant's compliments, sir, you need to see this."

"See what?" Cooper asked.

The boy swallowed and said, "Mr. Brim said that it was a hellish damn mess, Captain."

Everyone moved aside to let Cooper out, and then followed him topside. A young girl and boy, both naked, lay on the deck. Starvation, no water, and the sun had ravaged their young bodies. They were alive, but just barely.

Coop looked at T, who said, "I've sent for the surgeon's mate, Captain."

Kate walked up as T spoke. "Quickly," she said. "Get me two fresh sheets and a bucket of fresh water."

The sheets were laid out on the deck alongside each person. She wet the sheets, and rolled the girl first, and then the boy onto the sheets. She asked for two clean cloths. She wet the cloths and dripped water across their lips. She then folded the wet cloths and placed them over their eyes.

Kate then said, "Be careful and do not touch the skin any more than you have too. Let's get them down to sick bay." She looked at Midshipman Short, "Go see if the cook has any fresh grease or lard." With that being said, she followed the men carrying her two patients down to sick bay.

"Anything to identify the boat?" T called to Banty.

"They're pulling it up now," Banty replied.

When the bow came even with the rail, Ox grabbed it and singlehandedly pulled it on deck.

Lieutenant Dyea looked at Johannes. "Remind me not to anger that dear fellow."

Dagan laughed, "He's but a lamb."

Lieutenant Dyea smiled, "A lamb could be a baby ram."

When the boat was pulled around, faded out letters could be seen that said *Lucinda*.

"It appears that another ship has been taken," Dagan volunteered, and then turned away.

"Return to your ships," Cooper said to his captains. He laid his hand on Johannes' shoulder. "I want you to scout out Crooked Island. Do so at dark first. See if you can see any tell tale from your ship. If you feel comfortable make a pass off the northern tip during the day. For God's sake, don't let them take you, my friend. When you are finished, we'll rendezvous at Great Exuma. I want to look in at Spanish Wells. Ledford said a Negro spoke to one of his hands when they were at Eleuthera. He said that the bad men were at Spanish Wells."

"You have a care, Coop. I think that we are closing in on this Calico."

"Aye, so do I."

CHAPTER TWENTY TWO

IT WAS DARK WHEN the lookout spied her, their missing frigate. Banty was sure that it was her. Lieutenant James Drury seemed a bit skeptical that Banty could identify the ship in this light at their distance. Cooper and T had no such doubts. Banty had put Cooper on too many prizes during his pirate and privateering days to doubt the man, but he didn't think it was appropriate to mention it to Drury as most of the captured ships had been British.

T gave Coop a knowing look, when Coop said to the lieutenant, "I trust his sighting. He's never failed me yet."

They had just passed Sandy Point on Great Abaco when Banty spotted the frigate. "She is definitely headed in the direction of Spanish Wells and Eleuthera."

After parting with Johannes, Cooper had sailed to Freeport on Lieutenant Drury's suggestion. He felt that they might find a British frigate there and they could communicate with the ship, who could relay it on to Admiral Davy. However, luck was not on their side. The frigate, *Apollo*, of thirty-eight guns had been there patrolling the islands but had sailed for Antigua on Saturday. That would have been two days ago.

"We thought that they were going to sail on Friday as they finished taking on fresh water, but they waited and sailed on Saturday."

Drury smiled at this information. *Apollo's* captain, Peter Marrat, was not one to flaunt sailor's superstitions. Fridays were considered to be an unlucky day. No jacktar wanted to set sail on a Friday. Most captains tended to allow voyages to start on any day but Friday, so as to not upset the crew.

Cooper, using his glass, could see the stern lanterns in the distance. "Set more sail, T. I want to be up with that ship before we sight Spanish Wells."

"Aye, Captain."

Pipes sounded as the bosun sounded the call. As the cry to make more sail went up, the pounding of bare feet on the deck above caused the boy in sick bay to cry out and sit up. Kate was quickly at his side, reassuring him everything was fine and that he was being taken care of.

"Where's my sister?" he asked.

"She's here, you both have been burned by the sun and you're dehydrated," Kate responded.

"We wouldn't do what they wanted, so they set us adrift. They said the sun or the sea would do us in."

"Shh," Kate whispered. "I've given you some wine with a spoon of laudanum in it so that you can rest."

"My eyes," the boy said. "I can't see...my hands. Why are they tied?"

"Your hands are tied so that you don't cause more injury to yourself. There's a bandage over your eyes."

"Will I be able to see again," the boy asked.

Kate swallowed and took a deep breath. The truth is, she didn't know. "We'll see," she said.

"They didn't give us any water. They said to piss in our mouth if we got thirsty. We couldn't do that, it's not proper. He wanted us to do that. The Dandy. He made them strip us and when we were naked, he made us crawl around like dogs. He found out that Landis was my sister, so he wanted me to mount her like a dog. I refused to do that. He said that if I had sex with her, we could go free. I couldn't. He then wanted her to do lewd acts on him. Landis said no. Even when they cut her breast, she said no. The boy cut her breast with little knives on his fingers. It was the boy who said let the sea roast them."

Kate could scarcely believe what she was hearing. That the blackhearts would rape and torture adults was one thing, but children. The boy was maybe twelve or thirteen. His sister was a year or so older, fourteen at the most. The boy continued to mumble about the fancy boy with the knives on his fingers.

Kate mixed more wine and laudanum and gave it to the boy. "What's your name?" she asked.

"Mother...mother...," he cried out and then fell asleep.

Kate stepped out of the sick bay door and called for House, Josiah's assistant. When he came, she asked him to watch her patient a few minutes. She had to talk to the captain.

Dagan was in the captain's cabin with Cooper when she got there. They were discussing having the ship up to the frigate before dawn.

"Come in, Kate, and have a glass of wine."

"I need something stronger than wine," Kate said as she flopped into a chair.

"Josiah, a brandy for Kate, please."

Once she had the brandy, Kate took an unladylike gulp and downed half of it. She took a breath to calm herself and then related the boy's story. When she finished, Coop was up pouring more brandy.

Kate continued, "I fear that there's more as the boy was calling for his mother."

"They probably tortured and raped her in front of the boy," Coop said. "Maybe we'll catch him at Spanish Wells or Crooked Island."

Dagan shook his head. "We'll find pirates at both places. But his lair is not there. I felt that he was close when we found the first group on Marco Island." Dagan stood up shaking his head. Something was there, lying there just under the surface. But he had faced too many enemies to get a clear picture. He couldn't see like he did when he was younger. He tried to think of old enemies, yet the thought kept coming 'most of them are dead.' Did Marco Island hold the secret to who Calico was, or did his presence there just draw Dagan. If he could just go back maybe it would come to him. But no, there was no time for that. They had a ship to fight soon. He didn't want to cloud Cooper's thinking with a battle coming up.

***

IT WAS THE FRIGATE, *Syren*, as Banty had said. It was an hour before dawn and Brisco, the master, predicted a sunny day. Had the frigate still been in the Navy's hands, *Stag* would have been sighted long before now. *Stag's* crew had been sent to quarters in silence. Every gun had been made ready but the gun ports were still closed.

Spurlock, the gunner, passed his friend, Diamond, the bosun. "Have a care today, mate. They'll likely fight to the death before they give up."

"Aye, but as always, we have Cooper," Diamond replied.

"Aye, he's brought us more luck than anyone," Spurlock said, smiling. "To think, when Cap'n Taylor brought him on board, I had him pegged to be a Jonah."

"Yer not by yourself there, mate." Both men nodded and then went to their stations.

Lieutenant Drury stood by the ladder that would take him down to the gun deck. T was standing next to him when Cooper stepped over the coaming of the companionway and out on the deck. He was followed by Quang and Dagan. He'd gone down to get his pistols and sword. Quang had gone ahead, however, and met Cooper at the doorway to his cabin. He was now armed and ready to bring the pirates to battle and hopefully take possession of *Syren*.

Cooper paused a moment, thinking of Maddy and their unborn child. A quick prayer was said before he stepped out on deck. His cabin had quickly been torn down Navy fashion. It was something he had yet to get used to.

He saw the marines lined up and nodded a salute to Lieutenant Scott. "Have your sharpshooters ready today, Mr. Scott. I can promise you this band of cutthroats will not lay down their arms and surrender."

"Aye, Captain."

Cooper then greeted T and Lieutenant Drury. "Ready to wake up those blackhearts?"

"Aye," the two men said in unison.

"Mr. Short, are you the messenger?"

"Aye, Captain."

"Tell the gunner, then, that he may open this dance when he is ready."

"Yes, sir."

"Is it grape on top of ball, Lieutenant Drury?"

"Aye, Captain, as you ordered."

Cooper turned to T, "You have Spurlin positioned?"

"Aye, Captain, with two loaders."

Cooper still hadn't gotten used to T calling him, captain. It had always been Coop in the past. Of course, they'd never served on the same ship. T was now showing courtesy as protocol demanded.

Forward, the first bow chaser thundered out, followed closely by the second.

"If that didn't wake the sods, they are dead already," Banty said to Ox. The big man just smiled his big grin. Ox looked almost comical when he smiled, with his front teeth long missing from a fight.

"A hit," this was from Midshipman Shirreffs, who was at the fighting top.

Spurlock continued to blast away with the forward guns as *Stag* was nearly up to the frigate. Men were moving, in frenzy, on board the pirate ship. The pirates, taken by complete surprise, raced to the ship's guns to give battle.

Dagan watched as the frigate was slammed with ball after ball from *Stag's* guns. Pirates fell to the deck, kicking, screaming, and cursing as grape from the swivels rained down on them. Spurlock and the sharpshooters worked feverishly, but still some of the pirates made it to the ship's guns.

Cooper watched as a gun port opened, but before the gunners could fire, one of *Stag's* cannons thundered forth. The pirates' cannon was knocked back off its truck, killing several of the pirates as it was slammed by *Stag's* ball.

"Cease fire," Cooper called. "Cease fire."

The guns fell silent. Cooper, not wanting to destroy the frigate, picked up the speaking trumpet. "Do you surrender?"

"Go to hell," a pirate shouted back.

"Mr. Spurlin," Cooper called, "shoot that man."

BANG…a shot rang out and the man fell.

Cooper, taking the trumpet up again, asked once more, "Do you surrender?" No one answered. "You have thirty seconds to lay down your arms or you will all die."

A Negro pirate walked to the center of the deck and threw down his cutlass. A rogue standing in front of the gathered mob shot the black man in the back.

"Mr. Spurlin," Cooper called out.

BANG...the rogue fell writhing. Silence, an eerie silence.

"Shoot us now," one man said. "A ball now or a halter later, it's all the same."

Cooper wanted the frigate, and didn't want to lose anyone or cause more damage to the frigate. They had been very lucky so far. *Was it Dagan's lady luck?*

Regardless, Cooper made a quick decision, "You will be set free. I'll give you some ships' boats and a cask of water. Whether you live or die will be in God's hands."

The man who had spoken walked to the center of the deck and threw his blade on the deck. "It's a heart you have for the brethren, Cooper Cain. You were one of us once. I, for one, am glad it was you who caught us. But be prepared, Cooper. It's Satan himself who comes for you. Satan dressed in Calico. He's offered a thousand guineas to the man who brings you to him alive. Have a care, Cooper Cain."

CHAPTER TWENTY THREE

LIEUTENANT JAMES DRURY WENT over to their prize with a squad of marines, Dagan, Diamond, and Ox. The once beautiful British Naval frigate was a pig sty…worse.

There were several women on board, and those who chose to were put in a ship's boat with the pirates. There were others, women who were captives, and several men who had been put in chains. They were all freed. The men had value to the pirates, as they knew that a ransom would be paid for the prisoners.

A small chest of coins was found and in the captain's cabin a good supply of fine French wine.

Dagan said, "In the hole, there must be fifty casks of St. Croix rum. I saw no reason to cast it aside." Cooper smiled and thought, *nor would any member of his crew.*

Diamond took a crew over, and with the ship's carpenters and those from *Swan* and *Swallow*, *Syren* was pronounced ready to sail later that afternoon.

"I want to be off Spanish Wells at dawn," Cooper told Lieutenant Ludlow and Lieutenant Dyea of the *Swallow* and *Swan.* "Keep an eye out for ships that appear headed for the island. Take them if need be. I don't want the island to get word that we are in the area." Both captains acknowledged Coop's orders.

Ten men each from the *Swallow* and *Swan,* along with twenty men from *Stag,* went over to the recaptured frigate. Seven men who had been part of the pirate crew stayed with the ship.

They'd been taken at different times. They'd been given the option to join…or die, so they joined. All of them were British, except for one Canadian. Lieutenant Drury felt that they were telling the truth so he allowed the men to remain on board. Once they returned to Antigua, they could speak to the admiral about transportation home.

∗∗∗

"LAND HO!" THE CALL was just barely audible. *Swan* and *Swallow* had left formation an hour ago to take up a position below Russell Island. Cooper had T choose the men and assign the boat crews. Midshipman Shirreffs would be in charge of one boat. Ox would be with the boy to make sure no mistakes were made. The young mid, Shirreffs, had shown promise, much more than Midshipman Short, who had been sent over to *Syren* to help Lieutenant Drury.

Dagan had whispered to Shirreffs to look to the burly Ox for guidance if necessary, as he was an old hand at landing parties. He didn't mention that Ox's landings had been to pillage. There was no point in creating bias. Spurlock had the last boat. He took Spurlin with him. There was no one equal to the man with his long rifle.

Cooper finished his coffee and a piece of bread toasted with cheese. Josiah was forever amazing Cooper with his ability to come up with a fast easy meal when the elements or battle were in the offing. T would be in charge of *Stag* during the landing. Lieutenant Pitts would stay on board with him. He would stop or sink any ship or boat trying to make an escape on this side of the island.

Lieutenant Drury in the undermanned *Syren* would assist if needed. Hopefully, any idiot seeing two frigates would forget about trying to escape.

"The buggers are as drunk and careless as those on Marco," Cooper said to T as he went over the side and down to his waiting boat. As he went down, he suddenly thought of Maddy at home, alone and pregnant. Well, not really alone, her parents were there and Coop was sure that her best friend, Suzanne Bledsoe, was over several times a week.

What was it that Suzanne had said to him as he was leaving, 'You take care of yourself. You get yourself killed and leave Maddy a widow, I'll never speak to you again.' The thought made him chuckle.

Hearing the captain chuckle, a seaman quipped, "We's ready for another lark, Cap'n."

Cooper forced a smile. He wasn't sure this landing could be described as frolicking or playing but he hoped it would. They shoved off from *Stag* and rowed toward the beach. The sea had a gentle swell but thankfully nothing more. He didn't want the crew tired before they hit the beach.

✶✶✶

THE PIRATE WOKE UP. He'd passed out on the beach after finishing off a jug of rum. His bladder was sending a message to his brain that it needed immediate relief . His arm was numb and he couldn't raise it. A topless wench lay across his arm with her breasts pressed against him. His bladder was saying 'now or you will suffer a wet consequence.' Damn, the wench was heavy. However, with his bladder sending emergency signals to his brain, he none too gently snatched his arm from beneath the mammoth catheads pressed against his arm.

This roused the wench who snarled, "Have a care."

Walking a few feet toward the water's edge, the pirate had his manhood out, eyes closed and leaning back, he felt relief engulf him as he emptied his overextended bladder. "Ahh...," he groaned. Standing there, he heard a sound, and opened his eyes. There was something on the water. Rubbing his eyes, he leaned his head forward and squinted.

Boats…boats were landing. It could only mean one thing, at this time of the day, they had been found. The Navy or the pirate hunters were here. He ran back to the mound of sand where he'd been lying. The wench was back asleep. Shaking her, he said, "Wake up."

"Bugger off," came the reply.

The rogue gave a resounding, stinging slap across the woman's buttocks. The wench, covered by only a thin cotton dress, bolted upright with a dagger in her hand. "Slap me, will ye?"

"Shut up, you daft wench. We have trouble coming. Go wake up the others and tell them there are boats landing."

The woman looked around and found her blouse, grabbed it and put it on as she ran to spread the alarm. Seeing the boats clearly now as they beached, the pirate felt a sudden realization come over him. The island was about to be taken. He'd hang if he were captured. He was sure the pirates couldn't win when there was no telling how many ships were out there. To fight would likely end in death. To be captured would surely mean death. He'd thought of this a lot lately. He didn't like Calico or his lieutenant. They took pleasure in cruelty. He'd never liked it.

"To hell with them," he said. He had found a good hiding spot a few weeks ago. He'd stocked it with water and a bit of food. He'd make his way there now. Keeping down, he left the area. He would rather be stuck on the island than left hanging on the dock.

✳✳✳

A SHOT RANG OUT, followed by several shots. A ball thudded into the bow of the boat. Men ducked down, and no one was hit.

"Fire the swivel," Cooper ordered.

A gunner's mate, in the bow, slipped the tarp off the swivel. It had been loaded with grape before they left *Stag's* side. Once the tarp was removed, he adjusted the barrel to aim directly at the beach. Musket fire continued from the beach. The gunner's mate aiming at the last flash pulled the lanyard. The swivel let go with a loud bang and the gunner's mate was rewarded with a cry of pain followed by curses.

The boats on either side fired while the gunner's mate quickly reloaded his swivel. When he was finished, he looked at Cooper, who nodded. The swivel let go with another bag of grape, sending the balls buzzing to the beach. A few more cries were heard as the balls struck home. The pirates backed off now, retreating toward the interior of the island.

The landing parties were quickly out of the boats and formed up. They then moved out. They quickly came to a clearing where tents and grass huts had been set up. Someone fired a shot from one of the huts. A group of marines under a sergeant turned and fired into the hut. A woman ran out, blood pouring from her side. A man lurched to the door and then fell. The grass hut furnished no protection from the marines' balls, four of which had found the pirate's chest.

Cooper took his speaking trumpet to call on the rogues to surrender. A ball from a musket hit the trumpet and knocked it from Cooper's hand. A tell tale whiff of smoke drifted from a tree. Jimmy Spurlin took quick aim and fired. The sniper tumbled to the ground thudding into the sand. The pirates charged as if on signal, most of them preferring death in battle to the hangman. Cries and curses filled the air as the pirates charged. The marines and a few of the sailors got off one volley of shots, dropping five or six before the rest of the pirates were on them.

Cooper, with a cutlass in one hand and a pistol in the other, and his men prepared to meet the charge. Cooper shot the first rogue running at him. He dropped his pistol and pulled the dagger that Quang had given him years ago. He clashed swords with a man. With their blades locked, Cooper thrust in and down. The man dropped his blade and looked unbelievingly as his entrails fell from his abdomen as Cooper pulled his dagger free from the man's gut.

Quang had a bare-chested wench in a headlock as he fought off her man. He pivoted and slung the wench around at his attacker. The rogue's blade entered under the woman's arm. As she fell, her weight pulled the blade from the man's hand. Quang hacked at the man, his blade nearly splitting his foe.

Dagan stood on the stump of a tree. He had fired two pistols and was pulling another from his waistband. A third rogue fell dead at the base of the stump. Dagan's ball had entered his forehead, creating a third eye.

Shouts from men and women could be heard. The clang as metal blades came together could be heard also, and an occasional glint as the rising sun flashed on a clean blade could be seen.

Damme, Cooper thought, as more pirates joined the melee. *Where had these men been hiding?* He felt a jolt as he was hit in the back and knocked to his knees. He saw a blade sweeping down and was able to stop it from going home with his own. However, the impact of steel on steel jarred his arm so that he almost lost his grip on the blade. He rolled over, barely avoiding another attempt at killing him, and hearing the swoosh as the blade passed inches away from his head. The force of the swing was such that his attacker lost his balance and nearly fell. Cooper thrust up with his dagger, the blade entering his foe just below the sternum, puncturing a lung. The man cried out in pain and dropped to his knees, bloody foam coming from his mouth and nose.

Cooper worked his fingers as he grasped his blade. He could hear the marine sergeant bellowing out orders and then the deafening fire of muskets just to his left. Quang reached down and pulled Cooper to his feet.

A wench was trying to attack Ox, who kept telling her to stop. When she dove at him, both of her hands were trying to hold a much too heavy blade. Ox sidestepped the woman and slapped her a good one to the head. Whether dead from the blow or just knocked out, the woman dropped to the ground and didn't move.

The fight was suddenly over. The remaining blackhearts, few that they were, ran. Midshipman Shirreff, bruised and bloody, walked up to Cooper. "A victory I believe, Captain." Spurlock, who was behind the middy, smiled.

Cooper winked at Spurlock. "You are not wounded, are you, young sir?"

"Nothing serious, Captain, it is more their blood than my own."

"Good," Cooper replied. "Now if you will, Mr. Shirreff, assign a good man to find out our losses while another makes a quick inspection of the island to see what we can find."

"Aye, aye, Captain."

CHAPTER TWENTY FOUR

THE SIGHT OF ANTIGUA was a welcoming one, though Cooper wished it were Savannah. Dagan, puffing on a pipe and standing next to the fife rail spoke, "You'll be home before you know it, Coop."

It always amazed Cooper how Dagan seemed to know what he was thinking. "Being at sea seems to agree with you," Cooper responded.

"Aye," Dagan replied. "It's good to feel the wind, smell the tar, and taste the salt. There's nothing like it on land." *It also has awakened the senses*, Dagan thought, but didn't say. Things were coming to him like they did years ago.

The squadron, behind *Stag*, sailed into English Harbour, but unlike the last time, *Syren* was in the company, as well as a smart little Bermuda sloop that the pirates had taken.

The captain of the sloop, surprisingly, had not been killed as he had sworn that he could bring a thousand pounds in ransom money. But that had not kept his wife from being raped and abused by the pirates. A crewman told Spurlock that the man didn't seem to care what the pirates did to his wife. He seemed to enjoy it as she was stripped and tormented on deck in front of everyone. His name was Conway Kincaid, and he had demanded that he be put back in command of his own ship at once.

Lieutenant Ludlow had cleared his throat, getting Cooper's attention. Once they were alone, Ludlow spoke earnestly, "I wouldn't put him back aboard his ship, Captain. She was taken from him by the pirates. You have now taken her from them; therefore, the ship is a lawful prize. There will be no argument from the board. But if he resumes command, then the case is muddied as he can claim possession."

Cooper thanked Ludlow for the information, and then he told Kincaid that his request was denied. He'd be transported to Antigua aboard the *Syren*.

Midshipman Shirreffs, being the only midshipman now on board *Stag*, was the signals midshipman. He had his glass focused in on the flagship and was ready, therefore, when the signal was given. He rushed to where Cooper was standing next to Dagan. As firmly and official as he could make his voice sound, he said, "From flag, sir, captain repair on board."

"Well said, young sir," Dagan added after Cooper thanked him. Cooper thought the boy didn't realize what he had, having an old salt like Dagan taking a liking for him.

Kate Timberlake, acting surgeon's mate, stood by the entry port. She was going with Cooper to answer any questions that the admiral might have regarding the Westcoat family's capture by the pirates. The girl had finally come around enough to talk. Her name was Landis Westcoat, and her brother was Peter Westcoat. Their father had been Sir Edward Westcoat. Their mother's name was Emma. They had been en route to Grand Cayman where Sir Edward was to be the next governor. The girl had seen their father killed and their mother raped and sodomized. In desperation, her mother had yanked a knife from one of her tormentors and plunged it deep into his chest. Some of the other rogues had pulled him aside and shot her. Landis had seen all of this, but fortunately, Peter hadn't. He was spared that indignity, thank God.

Kate also needed to arrange to have Peter's eyes treated. He could see some now, but things were still blurry. She knew of some that had recovered from sun blindness, while others hadn't.

Cooper spoke to T, before going down to the boat below. "Secure the ship and put our third lieutenant in command of the ship until I return. It's time our Mr. Potts pulled his weight."

T smiled and thought to himself, Lieutenant Potts had pulled his weight and more.

✳ ✳ ✳

DOLCIE ANSWERED THE DOOR upon hearing a knock. Seeing her man, she exclaimed, "T, you're back." She was dressed in a nice dress and her hair was fixed nicely. A woman's voice, from inside, called, "Who is it, Dolcie?"

"It's T, madam," Dolcie replied.

Cooper's mother, Ann, came to the back door. "Is Cooper alright?"

"Aye," T responded. "He was summoned to the flagship to see the admiral as soon as we anchored."

A man walked in and Ann said, "Hear that, dear? Cooper has returned." Jean Paul smiled at his wife.

T looking at the man found it hard to believe that he was a master swordsman and once the best in France. He had been Cooper's teacher and if Cooper was to be believed, he could still slice a candle in half and never disturb the flame or topple it over. Of course, knowing of Cooper's prowess with a blade, T had no reason to doubt him.

"Come in, come in," Ann said adding, "get T some beverage, Dolcie."

T briefly explained their capture of several pirates and recovery of the frigate, *Syren*. He downplayed the battles, however once, he caught Jean Paul's eye and knew the man understood what had not been said.

After a cup of tea, Ann stood, "Dolcie, why don't you take the afternoon off? You and T need some time together."

Jean Paul stood, "I'll have Thomas bring the carriage around and we'll go down to the harbour. We might be able to catch Cooper."

When Ann turned to leave the room, Jean Paul gave T a wink. *He's leaving to give us time alone*, T realized. *Damned if the French were not romantics.*

T and Dolcie made small talk until the carriage pulled away. Dolcie rushed to him then and gave him a very warm, passionate kiss. When they broke apart, she pushed the door to her room shut and kissed T again, long and hot, her breath coming in gasps.

"Help me out of this damn dress," she whispered.

***

JAKE ANTHONY WELCOMED COOPER on board and said, "The admiral is waiting." Cooper quickly explained about Kate.

Jake called a lieutenant over, "Take Mrs. Timberlake to see the surgeon. Give him my regards and tell him to offer her every courtesy." He whispered to Cooper, after seeing Kate, "Once the sod sees her, he'll be falling all over himself to help."

Coop smiled, "Aye, she knows how to lay on the charm when needed."

Admiral Davy rose from his desk and, taking Cooper's hand, offered him a warm and friendly greeting. Cooper thought he is probably glad that we have his ship back.

Cooper was offered a glass by the admiral's servant. He then sat down and gave a good summary of what he'd been able to do and find out, taking the frigate *Syren* back, raiding the pirates and freeing several captives. When he got to the point of the murder, rape, and torture of Sir Edward Westcoat and his wife, the admiral had his flag lieutenant go get Mrs. Timberlake.

While they were waiting on Kate to appear, a commotion was heard on deck. A man was saying that if he wasn't taken to the admiral instantly, the lieutenant would rue the day.

"I'll go," Jake said. A few minutes later, Jake's voice could be heard, "Damme man, do you realize that you are on a flagship, and not some bumboat? You spit on my deck again and I'll personally throw your arse over the side."

Admiral Davy and Cooper looked at each other smiling. "Jake takes pride in the ship's appearance," Davy said, smiling.

***

GOVERNOR BASNIGHT MET WITH Admiral Davy and Cooper that afternoon. While the governor was pleased with Cooper's progress, he was saddened by the news of Sir Edward Westcoat and his wife's murder.

"I have known Sir Edward since our school days," he said. Basnight called a servant and had him fetch his wife. "We will go bring the children here," he said. "We are well known to them."

Governor Basnight looked at Cooper, before concluding the meeting. "I have a note here from a Mister Warren Kincaid making harsh statements against you, Cooper." Smiling, the governor looked at Admiral Davy. "He also states some Navy officer threatened him with bodily harm. Who would like to speak first?"

"I will," Admiral Davy said, "since Cooper acted upon the advice of one of my officers."

Basnight listened and said, "It seems straight forward to me." He then paused and said, "Did Jake really threaten him with bodily harm?"

"If tossing his arse in the harbour is bodily harm, then I guess he did."

"Hmm...and what offense did Kincaid commit to receive such a threat?"

"The man cleared his throat and spat on the ship's deck, not once but twice. In front of witnesses, I might add."

"I see, sir," Robert said. "So…in essence he was defacing government property."

"I believe that is so," the admiral said.

"I've also got a letter from Kincaid's wife stating the man basically encouraged the blackhearts to take their pleasure in raping and torturing her. She also relates that she has several witnesses who will swear that he told the pirate captain to do with her as they wished, as long as he was left unharmed for ransom."

Cooper spoke, "I'm not sure where this is going, sir, but there are several who have said that Mr. Kincaid took pleasure in watching his wife being demeaned."

The governor shook his head. "The lady says that Kincaid married her for money but she didn't realize it until it was much too late. Her father is on the board of the Honest Johns, and that in itself means that her family has money. She is asking for charges to be brought against the man for attempting to bring about her murder in hopes of personal gain. She is also petitioning for a divorce."

"Do you have the authority?" Admiral Davy asked.

"I don't know. It may be easier to make her a widow. I can bring charges for his attempt to have his wife murdered, if the witnesses' statements support it."

"I don't think that will be hard," Cooper said. "I'm sure that his entire crew would side with the wife."

A servant knocked on the door and announced Sir Robert's wife. Sir Robert then invited Cooper, along with his parents and any other guests that he would like to bring to dinner that night. He also invited the admiral and Ariel, as well as Jake Anthony.

CHAPTER TWENTY FIVE

A HARD RAIN SLANTED FORCEFULLY, coming out of the west and driven by a hard wind. Overhead dark clouds seemed to race across the sky. As *Stag* tugged at her anchor cables, Cooper looked at Dagan.

Dagan swatted at something, a fly or some pesky insect. Once the pest was driven away, Dagan spoke, "Brisco says the blow will not last long."

Cooper snorted as another white cap crashed into *Stag's* hull. "It doesn't take long to be driven onto the shore." Dagan smiled at his comment.

Cooper wanted to be away. He wanted to put an end to this pirate business and be home with Maddy. Jake's actions the previous night probably had a lot to do with it.

Admiral Davy and his wife, Ariel, had hosted a dinner for the squadron's captains and first lieutenants. Ariel, who was Dagan's ward, had touched his arm and said, "Look there, Father."

Captain Jacob Anthony entered, escorting Katharine (Kate) Timberlake. Kate had once again transformed her appearance. Neither Cooper nor Dagan could imagine the hardened woman in seaman's slops asking to be taken on as a surgeon's mate was this beautiful creature on Jake's arm. She had been a doctor's wife who'd watched her husband being murdered and she had then been raped repeatedly. She now showed no sign of the travesty. Even in seaman's slops, she'd turn men's heads. But in this evening gown, she was one of the most beautiful women that Cooper had ever seen, second only to Maddy.

She wore a dark blue gown cut low enough so that you could see the swell of her breasts, but not so low as to be scandalous. Her sun streaked blonde hair made the dress a perfect match. She wore an emerald necklace that made you want to touch the throat it hung around. Her matching earrings dangled and caught the flames from the candles overhead. After a moment, Cooper realized the outfit belonged to his mother. She had made sure that Kate was coiffured and dressed to impress.

Dolcie and T came in then. Cooper's mother had played the mother hen, making sure the women would be the talk of the evening. Dolcie was dressed in a peach colored outfit with a pearl necklace and earrings.

Cooper had invited his mother and Jean Paul to visit *Stag*. She had met Kate there, and of course, Dolcie lived at their home.

As Dagan and Cooper listened to the wind and rain on deck, Dagan spoke again, "I see a couple of weddings in the future."

Cooper thought for a moment, "I can see T and Dolcie, but Kate and Jake? Do you think that she's over her ordeal this soon?"

Dagan smiled, "We'll see."

✳✳✳

FULLY PROVISIONED, INCLUDING EXTRA provisions for *SeaFire*, Cooper's squadron of pirate hunters set sail the following day. Seeing Kate by the fife rail, Dagan walked over. "Thinking of a gallant sea captain?" Dagan asked.

"No, I was thinking of those children that we left with Sir Robert and his wife. I hope that they find peace," Kate responded.

"And you as well," Dagan said, speaking softly.

Kate put her hand on Dagan's leathery hand. "Yes, a sea captain was in my thoughts as well. He is your nephew?"

"Aye," Dagan replied. "He comes from a long line of sea officers. His grandfather, his father and uncle were all admirals."

Kate let a fleeting smile cross her face. "You are saying that I'll always have to share him with the sea, if it goes that far." There was a glimpse of a smile again. "He knows how I was...taken. Taken and used. He put his finger on my lips to stop me from talking, and then he kissed me. My past mattered not."

"Nor should it," Dagan said.

A tear ran down Kate's cheek. "I never thought that a man, a gentleman would want me knowing what I've been through."

Dagan wiped away Kate's tears with his handkerchief, and then kissed her forehead. "A real man wouldn't care," he whispered.

A real smile came to Kate's face, this time. "Is it hard to share your man?" she asked.

Dagan smiled and said, "Now, that's a question you would have to ask Faith or Maddy."

"Sail ho!" The lookout's cry broke up the conversation.

"Thank you," Kate mouthed as she walked away.

Cooper was on deck soon. He asked for his glass when the lookout called down again, "She be *SeaFire*."

"I knew that Johannes would be at the rendezvous," Cooper said.

The two ships closed and, while the provisions were being taken across, Johannes sat in Cooper's cabin enjoying a glass of hock.

"They are there alright," Johannes said. "My first pass was at night. I had men aloft. They reported at least a dozen fires. I sailed a full day into the Windward Passage before coming about to make my second pass. Again, I had several lookouts aloft. It's a perfect spot for the pirates, but one that has to be supplied. The French Wells is sheltered by the cays between

Long Cay and Crooked Island." Pausing for a swallow of wine, Johannes wiped his mouth with a cloth and continued. Pointing at the chart, he said, "The shallow flats here keeps ships from boxing in the blackhearts."

"You mean the Bight of Acklins," Brisco asked as he poured over the best chart on the area that he had.

"Aye," Johannes responded. "Ships anchored in this area," Johannes pointed at the passage between Crooked Island and Long Cay, "are nearly impossible to spot. So when a likely ship passes, it is nothing for the pirates to come out and attack a merchant ship before they realize that they are in trouble."

Wrapping up his report, Johannes said, "Is that a new addition to our force?" He was speaking of the frigate.

"Aye, she's the *Phallas* of thirty-two guns." Cooper then went on to tell of the sighting and the recapturing of the *Syren* and attacking Spanish Wells, and then returning to Antigua.

Johannes listened and said, "I don't think Crooked Island will be as easy, Coop. There's a landing of sorts at Pitts Town and a sandy beach for most of the island that we saw. The old fort and plantation house are west of Pitts Town. There's a tower at the fort, probably used for observation when the Redcoats Army was there."

Cooper smiled; Johannes was letting his American bias show in his choice of words...Redcoats.

CHAPTER TWENTY SIX

THE MOON WAS ONLY a sliver on the horizon when boats pushed off from the squadron's ships. The wind was slight and gentle rollers found their way onto the beaches. If anyone had been watching, it would seem an invasion force was landing to take the island...it was.

After calling his captains together to plan the attack, Cooper agreed with Captain Sartain of *Phallas*. Since the number of pirates and their state of readiness might be more than they'd previously encountered, this attack might need to be multi pronged. The land force would land, make ready and signal *Phallas* with three flashes from a striker. Upon seeing the signal, *Stag* and *Phallas* would start firing on the fort using the bonfires as targets. After twenty minutes, the barrage would lift and Cooper's force would attack. *Stag's* marine commander, Lieutenant Scott, would lead the marines from the east.

Cooper's force, with half of the sailors, would work their way around the encampment and attack from the west side. T, along with *Phallas's* First Lieutenant Underwood, would attack from the rear. Midshipman Shirreffs and a midshipman from *Phallas* would act as messengers.

Before they left *Stag*, T grinning, said to Cooper, "Mr. Potts has assumed his role as Captain. Look at the quarterdeck."

Cooper smiled, "Let him have his moment. It will look good in his record that the Navy is so fond of."

T replied, "It's a good thing that Brisco will have charge of the helm and Spurlock the guns."

"Shhh…" Cooper hissed. "Here he comes.

Potts saluted Cooper just before Cooper went over the side. "Good hunting, Captain."

"Thank you, Mr. Potts. Hopefully we will."

Once Cooper was in the boat, Dagan whispered, "You've made his day."

"Make room for the captain," young Shirreffs growled as Cooper got in his boat. When he went to take a seat aft by Cooper, Quang moved in front of him. If there was any doubt who would be next to the captain, it was quickly resolved. One look at the big Chinaman had the mid nodding slightly to the cox'n and sitting on the next seat.

The marines landed first. Lieutenant Scott set up a defensive line and sent out a few scouts. By the time the other boats had landed, it was four a.m.

"It's not long until dawn," Dagan whispered.

Since Cooper's group had the most distance to cross, he had Shirreffs with the woodsman, Jimmy Spurlin, go with T's group. Once they were ready, they'd make for Cooper's group and the signal would be sent. Moving through the dark, the men miraculously were able to set up without alerting the pirates that they were there. None of the weapons had been loaded to avoid a gun from going off if someone fell. There would be plenty of time to load the guns after the ship's guns started firing.

When Cooper was finally in place, he found a dune that was higher than the rest and sent Quang atop it to be ready to send the signal when Shirreffs and Spurlin showed up. The moments seemed to last forever. Cooper felt for his watch and started to take it out, but changed his mind and just patted the pocket. He was a case of nerves but didn't want the men to pick up on it.

Dagan touched his shoulder and pointed. It was Spurlin and the middy.

"All's ready, Captain," Shirreffs said.

Cooper nodded to the Chinaman. Was it growing lighter or were his eyes becoming more accustomed to the darkness? As a precaution, every man who landed wore a white armband. When the fighting started, Cooper didn't want a man from another ship taken for a foe. Even though the firing was expected, the men jumped when the first salvo went off. The orange flames that leapt from the cannon's mouth was as spell bounding as it was frightful.

The ground shook as balls rained down, sending vast amounts of dirt and debris flying into the air. Some of the balls found pirates' huts and tents. Others slammed into the rock walls, sending sharp rock fragments into a mass of frightened pirates. Balls rained down, causing mass hysteria and confusion.

Cooper ordered his men to load their weapons. It wouldn't be long before the pirates would seek a way to escape the hell that was falling on them. Midshipman Shirreffs turned his head as a ball fell on a running pirate, sending arms and legs in different directions.

Dagan placed his hand on the youth and whispered to him. Cooper couldn't hear what was said but the boy looked up at Dagan and nodded.

A group of the pirates tried to escape by running down the beach toward Pitts Town. They were met with musket balls as the marines poured it on. Only a few cracks of fire were heard, as the ships' cannons drowned out their sound, but the short stabs of light from the musket barrels showed up plainly. It all ended then. The cannons fell silent. Pirates turned to look toward the sea, not believing the hell was over…it wasn't.

Cooper then yelled, "Quickly before they can regroup."

T had thought the same thing. From behind the pirates, a savage screaming hoard was coming at them. Muskets and pistols fired into the pirates as the sailors ran forward to engage the confused pirates. Sailors and marines attacked, jumping over the debris, and lifeless bodies. To the pirates it seemed like an endless wave. Some of the pirates ran, and some of them raised their hands, but others gathered around a man as big as Quang, and were mounting a defense.

T's group was the first one to meet this group. It was a fierce melee. Men fought hand-to-hand. It was win or die, so the pirates gave as good as they got for a few minutes. Good men fell. Johannes had been right - these pirates would not be taken easily.

Shouts, curses, and cries of pain filled the air. A man spat into T's face and cursed him, the curse dying on his lips as T's blade severed the rogue's carotid artery, blood spurting out as he fell. T wiped his face and dispatched another man. The sheer number of sailors overwhelmed the pirates, and many died as two or three sailors at a time, plunged their blades into the blackhearts.

T then faced the giant. He was Axel de Corsia, and was the last pirate making a fight of it. No introductions were made, but T knew it was the Ax. As he faced the big man, T felt a stab and a sharp pain in his groin area. He kicked out reflexively, breaking the jaw of a small man, a midget. His eyes had been on the Ax and somehow the little sod had stabbed him. It was much like the Westcoat children had described. The man had devised small knives or blades that fit over his fingers. The little man, with his jaw hanging loose at an odd angle, worked his fingers as the razor sharp blades glinted in the firelight. The man let out a scream and dove at T, but Ox swung his cleaver of a blade, severing an arm, and blood started pouring from the stump. The man looked down at his lifeless hand and bent over to pick it up. He never made it as he fell dead, and de Corsia cursed.

"T," Cooper called.

Ax was twice the size of T, but T looked at Coop and said, "He's mine."

The men stood back and gave them some room. Spurlin volunteered, "I can put a ball between his eyes."

Ax had been standing on a section of fence that had been hit by the bombardment. Cooper could see a widening dark spot on T's britches. He was bleeding from the midget's blades. He would be too weak for a long fight.

"Let them fight," Cooper said to Spurlin, "but if Ax hurts T, shoot the son of Satan."

Ax leaned over and picked up a boarding ax. Spinning the ax in his hand, the bloodstains of its victims were obvious. T deftly caught the dagger with the ivory horse head handle that Cooper tossed him.

The two men circled as the dawn light rose in the faint morning mist . De Corsia swung the boarding ax and then jerked it back. The blade missed but the spike dug into T's shirt, leaving a thin red furrow. T felt the sting and knew that he was lucky he'd reared back when he did or he'd be dead with his ribs and sternum torn from his chest. He'd learned something though. When de Corsia had ripped backwards, he was off balance and left himself wide open. De Corsia circled again, and this time he swung the ax and plunged with the blade. The man was a master. There was a smile on his face and his eyes seemed to gleam.

T had easily ducked the ax but the blade had sunk into his shoulder. He felt a burning, searing pain and felt blood run down his arm to his hand and onto the dagger handle. De Corsia circled again, making little advances with his blade. Metal clanged on metal. As T watched, de Corsia's eyes widened as this time he thrust with the blade, followed by swinging the ax. Both men missed their targets.

"Lucky," de Corsia hissed as he circled again.

T easily deflected his foe's feinting attacks with the blade. De Corsia's eyes then widened and he took a deep breath, causing his chest to swell. He struck, but T was ready.

T fell back on the sand, rolled and slashed, severing Axel the Ax de Corsia's Achilles tendon. The man fell backwards onto the sand. T was on his knees and when his man fell, he plunged down with all his might, driving his blade through de Corsia's chest and out his back. Disbelief filled the fallen man's face for just a moment. He tried to speak but frothy blood gushed from his mouth. He reached upward with a hand, his fingers pointing to the sky. His hand dropped, and the man was dead.

CHAPTER TWENTY SEVEN

THE SUN SHONE DOWN bright as wounded men, including T, were taken back to their ships. Those that had not survived were counted and their names noted so that they could be entered "discharged dead" on the ships' books.

A few people who had cringed in fear during the bombardment, made their way to the battleground. Many were lending a hand with the wounded.

"God bless you, Captain," one man said. "You've removed a terrible blight from the island. You have no way of knowing the fear that we've lived under. We've had to feed the scoundrels and none of our women were safe. We've managed to slip some of our younger women and girls over to Acklins. Thank God they never searched over there."

Once the final count was made, there were over one hundred pirates dead. Cooper's force had fourteen wounded, of which most were thought likely to live. They had lost ten men, though. Some would consider it a minimal loss, but not Cooper. Some of them he'd known for years...back when they'd been pirates themselves. There were perhaps thirty-five captives. Most of them were women, and of those, a large number were girls fourteen or younger.

It was a girl of twelve who offered the only possibility as to where Calico might be. While she was forced to touch herself in lewd ways, Calico had asked one of his boys if he wanted to take her to Dead Man's Bay to play with.

"No, she's too skinny," the boy had declared. "Let's let her mature some more." During all that time, he let the knives on his fingers circle her tiny breasts and abdomen.

The women had been kept naked, so they didn't appear bothered that they were nude until blankets were produced to cover themselves. They gratefully wrapped themselves then. There were only five men with the captives, and they were being held for ransom. They had been able to keep their britches, but nothing else, not even their shoes. Most of the men were elderly, and one of them was known to Cooper. He was Merriweather Woodham, and Cooper had last seen the man during the war. Cooper had taken the man's ship, but as the man's daughter, Kathleen, had been on board, he'd let the man keep the ship. Kathleen had been a close friend of the twins and himself back in their youth. She would bring a great ransom from her father, so why did Calico take her?

"Cooper, there was something familiar in the rogue's voice," Merriweather said.

"Which rogue?" Cooper asked.

"The leader of these whoresons, the man who took Kathleen," Merriweather said exasperation in his voice. The man was more used to people jumping at his every whim. Now he was trying to tread in a totally new environment. One in which all sense of dignity and self-respect had been torn away by the pirates, and particularly their leader.

Merriweather was now free, but rattled. He indicated that their ship had been taken off of Bermuda over a month ago. Ransom demands had been sent to their families. His son surely had had time to make payment. The thought of his son not doing so was very disturbing to Merriweather, shaking his faith in his son.

"Please forgive my behavior, Cooper. I've been humiliated and now doubts rise up as to my son's love and loyalty."

Cooper said to the old gentleman, "These things take time, sir. If payment had been made the day the demand was delivered, it has hardly had time to have gone through the chains to reach Calico."

"Thank you, Cooper, for trying to salve an old man's feelings, but we both know the truth. I am thankful that you have rescued us."

The old man was still speaking when the thunderous boom of ships' cannons were heard. BOOM…BOOM!!

"Quang, get up in that tower and see what's happening."

Quang climbed the wooden ladder to the top. While still holding onto a rung, he peered out. "Ship try to sail away," he shouted down. *Stag* and *Phallas* fire on it. *Swan* and *Swallow* going alongside the ship." The Chinaman's short, blunt sentences told the story.

Seeing Midshipman Shirreffs, Cooper called to him. "Have Marine Lieutenant Scott report to me."

"Aye, Captain."

Since T was wounded, Cooper called to Lieutenant Underwood, *Phallas'* First Lieutenant, "Take your party and half of the marines and head toward the bay at the western tip of the island. See if there are any more ships at anchor. If Dagan is up to the hike, ask him to go along."

"Excuse me, Captain." It was Banty speaking.

"Yes," Cooper replied.

"I believe Dagan took the child, Isabella, to the ship when they took T."

"Alright, Banty, you go. You know how to do the type of search I'm after."

"Aye, Cap'n. Diamond be around also."

"Good, take him," Cooper said. Feeling that he owed Lieutenant Underwood an explanation, he said, "These men have experience sniffing out hiding places that the average person would never consider."

Lieutenant Underwood smiled. "Experience gained searching for British ships back in your privateering days, no doubt," he said. The smile let Cooper know that there was no resentment.

"Aye," Cooper replied, smiling back.

Quang walked up to Cooper. "Boat ready to go to ship. You go, you stay?"

Cooper looked around and saw that all of the captives had been taken off the island. A search was being made for any pirates who may have gotten away. Most of the pirates' muskets and pistols had been given to the people of Pitts Town to defend themselves if one or more rogues showed up after Cooper's ships had departed. Lieutenant Underwood would send word once he found anything. Pirates were being rowed out to the waiting ships, to be taken to Antigua for trial.

Cooper would have hung them there, but the governor seemed to want some of them to be taken to Antigua, tried and executed by the government. Well, he had, at least, forty or fifty pirates for the governor to do with as he wished.

Cooper still didn't have Calico, however. To his mind, the job wouldn't be complete until that devil of a man had been brought to justice.

❊❊❊

THE GIRL, ISABELLA, WAS brought to Cooper's cabin by Kate. Dagan was already there. When they arrived, Josiah brought out a plate of cookies and sweetened lemon juice. Seaman slops had been given to the girl. They'd been pinned up but were still much too large. Sitting down and diving into the cookies she wrinkled her nose and spoke, "These are the best. I've not had anything near so good in a long time." Her next comment surprised Cooper and caused Josiah to raise his gentleman's eyebrow. "Thank you for these clothes, but I'd be much more comfortable if I could take them off. Being naked was much better…even if society doesn't approve. All the girls and all the boys have the same thing, so why do we have to wear scratchy clothes?" Everyone smiled at this.

"We've talked about this, dear," Kate said. Obviously Kate had tried to impress upon the girl the need to cover her naked body. Kate spoke then, "Isabella watched as her mistress was abused, mutilated, and murdered. The husband was killed fighting for his wife."

Cooper nodded his head and said, "Now, Isabella, you said that you talked to the leader of the pirates."

"Yes," she said, chewing on a cookie.

"Could you tell us about him?" Cooper asked.

"He changed clothes every day. One day it was yellow, the next day it was green."

"Yes," Cooper acknowledged. "Aside from the color of his clothes, tell me about him."

"He always wore everything the same color. His hats all had a veil on them, and it looked like silk lace. He wore a monocle on a gold chain. I saw him lift the veil to fix the monocle to his eye. His face was badly scarred. His ear was missing and I didn't see any eyebrow. He looked over at me but I was holding my head down so he didn't see me looking. He doesn't like for people to look at him. His boy used his finger knives and cut a woman's guts out when she looked at him. Her intestines fell on the floor. He made her pick them up and carry them out of the hut. When I went out, she was dead."

"Was there anything else that you noted about him?"

"He wore white gloves, because on one hand there were no fingers and on the other hand there was only a thumb and the first finger. He had sticks or crutches but they didn't fit under his arms. The pads seemed to fit about here," the girl said, pointing at her forearms.

"Is there anything else that you can tell me?" Cooper asked.

"When anybody, any of the captives go in front of him, they have to be stripped. The big pirate, Ax, and only a couple more, besides his boys, are allowed close to him. They form a circle around him whenever there's a big get together."

CHAPTER TWENTY EIGHT

THE TRIP BACK TO Antigua was uneventful. Lieutenant Underwood found two more ships. One was a converted merchant ship that carried twenty guns, the other a schooner that carried ten guns. The schooner was named the *Blue Caribee*. She was reasonably clean, making Cooper think that she'd only recently been taken by the pirates. De Corsia had been the captain of the ex-merchant ship. They'd never removed the stern plate naming the ship the *Morning Rose*. They'd just painted a word over it in black...*Fang*. Someone had attempted to add a serpent head, but it was a poor likeness.

The ship was better kept than most of its kind. De Corsia had kept a log of ships that they'd taken. Other than the names of the ships, the other details were sketchy. The details were listed as good cargo for resale.

De Corsia had written, 'This will please Calico. There are two men for ransom and enough women to keep the bloaks happy.' Bloak...that term usually identified a British or Irish man, and de Corsia was French. Dagan had suggested that it was probably a British secretary.

The entry for when the Woodham ship was taken read, 'The ship owner is worth some ransom. His daughter is worth one hundred pounds, at least, but may become Calico's plaything.' From what Cooper had discovered, Calico's playthings didn't fare well for very long. Hopefully, Kathleen was still alive, although death might be preferable based on the information that they had gained.

T was on deck as the ships entered English Harbour. A thought occurred to Cooper, "T, have you plans for when this is over?"

T looked at his friend. "I've got some thoughts, but nothing definitive yet."

"I think that our job is close to being finished, T. Unless something new arises, I don't foresee us returning to Antigua but one more time. If you want to continue being at sea..." Before Coop could finish his sentence offering T a ship, T shook his head.

"No, Coop, I think I'm done with the sea. I may try my hand at farming," T replied.

Coop smiled, "Would Georgia be a likely place to make you try?"

"It's as good as any I suppose," T responded.

Coop nodded his head and said, "Are you considering a permanent relationship with Dolcie?"

"Aye, but we've not really discussed it."

"Discuss it with her, T. If she's amenable, tell her to tell my mother and be ready to go when we return."

"I'll do it," T said.

✹✹✹

ON BOARD THE FLAGSHIP, *Minotaur*, the lieutenant on duty reported to his captain. It was not the most official sounding report Flag Captain Jacob "Jake" Anthony had ever received, but it covered the facts.

"Pardon me, Captain, but the lookout has sighted the *Stag* entering port. Coop's entire squadron is with him and they've taken three more prizes."

"Good news," Captain Anthony responded. "I will inform the admiral." As he went to inform Admiral Davy, he thought, *it will be good to see Coop, but it would be great to see Kate.* The smile was still on Jake's face, as he was entering the admiral's cabin.

Cooper reported to Admiral Davy the success of their latest action. "I've a feeling," Cooper said, "that we've decimated the pirates so that their ability to attack our shipping is by all accounts over."

He had questioned the pirate prisoners at length. They all agreed that unless Calico had ships that were unbeknownst to them, all the pirate ships had been taken. Calico had a ten gun Bermuda sloop. No one used it but him. He had his own crew made up mostly of freed slaves. He rarely ever stayed over at one of the rendezvous points more than a night, unless de Corsia was there.

Coop went on to explain the latest group of British subjects, including his old friends' father, Merriweather Woodham, and the girl who preferred to be naked rather than wear clothes. Cooper then reported what he knew regarding the possibility of Calico's lair. He described what Isabella had told them about the man's deformities. He also told of Calico's pleasure in torturing and disfiguring his captives. He ended his report by saying that Merriwether Woodham thought that Calico's voice sounded familiar to him.

Admiral Davy sent his flag lieutenant to get the ship's master and have him bring any charts dealing with Deadman Bay. The master soon reported, but was embarrassed to say that he had no charts of such a place.

Cooper was not surprised. *I need to talk with Eli Taylor,* he thought. *If anybody knows where the place is, it would be Eli.* Thinking of the trip home and seeing Maddy made Cooper feel suddenly better.

The constant stress of hunting down the pirates had weighed heavily on him. Was it because Maddy was pregnant? Regardless, he would see her soon.

"I will inform the governor of your actions and of your prisoners. By the way, Coop, it seems Mr. Kincaid, the man whose ship you took and whose wife wanted him charged with attempted murder, was found dead behind one of the island's roughest taverns. His throat was slit, and his manhood had been cut off.

"A woman's scorn," thought Cooper aloud.

"Possibly," the admiral replied. "But what man would take pleasure in seeing his wife humiliated by pirates?" The statement didn't need an answer.

"I guess Sir Robert has to mount an investigation."

"I suppose so, once he has time and, of course, trying these pirates takes precedence," the admiral responded.

Coop smiled, "I'm sure."

CHAPTER TWENTY NINE

THERE WERE ONLY TWO ships that sailed away from Antigua. With the thought being that the pirate threat was essentially over, the naval ships were put back to regular naval service. A party was held for Cooper on board the flagship. The captains of *Swan* and *Swallow* were very verbal in their praise and appreciation of Cooper. They were younger men, who had not yet developed rigid mindsets. Hopefully, they would survive and become good commanders.

Cooper had visited his mother and Jean Paul. After telling them about Isabella's mistress being murdered, Cooper's mother said if the girl had no one whom she wanted to go back to England for, she would give the girl a trial. Coop japed about making sure Isabella understood about wearing clothes.

Dolcie said that she'd be ready to leave with T when he next returned. In the meantime, she would assist Cooper's mother in reintroducing Isabella to the need to be covered up...at least in public. This drew laughs from the group.

Kate had been at the dinner as Jake Anthony's guest. The two spent most of the week together and one night she'd not returned to Coop's mother's house, where she'd been staying while the ship was in port.

The next day had been Cooper's farewell party on board the flagship. Jake had taken Cooper aside and told him that he'd asked Kate to marry him. "She didn't say yes, but she said to let her think about it. She said, 'It's not been that long since my husband was murdered. I loved him dearly, Jake. I don't think it would be fair to you to say yes, and then not be the wife you need me to be.' She also said 'I do think that I love you, Jake, I just need some time.'"

They had spent the night together, but they'd not made love. He held Kate the entire night, and she was still asleep when he'd slipped away to get dressed.

She came to him as he was about to leave and asked, "Are you disappointed that we didn't make love?" Jake looked at Coop, and said, "I lied, Coop, I said no. How could I be disappointed when I was holding her?"

"What did she say?" Coop asked.

"She said that I was a liar…a sweet liar but a liar."

Jake and Cooper both laughed, and then went into the admiral's cabin to join the others.

✱✱✱

THE VOYAGE FROM ANTIGUA went well. The skies were clear and the wind held fairly constant between a gentle and moderate breeze. They'd spotted one naval vessel, which closed within hailing distance, and they passed the latest news. The ship had sailed out of Antigua the day after Cooper's squadron had arrived. The naval vessel was a sloop of war, the *Sting*, of ten guns.

Lieutenant Seymour was the captain. "Did you clear the seas, Captain Cain? I saw the ships that you brought in as we were getting underway."

"I think that we got most of them," Cooper replied. "What rogue has a chance when we fine fellows give chase?"

"Well said, Captain Cain. Fair winds to you, sir."

Cooper threw up his hand and answered, "You as well, sir."

The man surprised Cooper then, "I'll tell Admiral Anthony that I saw you when we return to port."

"Do that," Cooper said, as the *Sting* sailed away.

As soon as the ship was beyond hearing distance, Cooper called to T, "The pirates have that ship."

T and those close by looked in awe at Cooper. "How do you know?" T asked.

"Lieutenant Seymour said that he'd tell Admiral Anthony. He knew that I'd know that it's Admiral Davy, who is in command. Jake Anthony is the flag captain, not the admiral. Signal for *SeaFire* to close, Mr. Shirreffs."

"Banty," Cooper then called.

"Aye, Cap'n."

"Go aloft and keep your eyes on that ship. I want to know what her direction is."

When *SeaFire* closed to hailing distance, Cooper explained to Johannes about his fears. He told Johannes to sail to larboard, but not out of sight, and said, "A strike in the night means close with the other ship."

Johannes held up his hand in acknowledgment. A strike or spark at night could be seen a long ways at sea. Especially if one was expecting to see it.

Stag came about, as did *SeaFire*, taking a course on *Sting*, and they continued to follow her.

Banty confirmed the ship was continuing on the same course until it became to dark to see. Cooper was about to bring his lookout down when Banty called out.

"They've lit their stern lights, Captain."

T looked at Cooper, "Is it a ploy?"

"They're trying to keep up appearances of a British warship," Dagan said. "It's normal to have the stern lights lit unless at war."

Coop shook his head, "We'll keep a dark ship, T."

"Aye, Captain."

Cooper thought a moment and then added, "Let's make all sail, T. Hopefully, we will be up on her before she knows it."

"Aye, Captain," T repeated.

All hands were called with the shrill of bosun's pipes. Men went to their stations and when all the sails had been clamped on, Cooper ordered an extra ration of rum. When the men had their rum and had been fed, Cooper and Dagan went below.

Josiah had cold meat slices and cheese ready. "I didn't think that you'd want anything too heavy, Captain."

"Thank you, Josiah, I appreciate your thoughtfulness."

Dagan and Cooper discussed how the pirates could have taken control of a British sloop of war.

"I'm sure that we'll find out when we take her," Cooper said.

"Aye, if any of the ship's company survives to tell us," Dagan responded.

It was midnight but the bell didn't ring out. Cooper stood on the quarterdeck, with Quang just behind him, and Dagan stood at his side. They had closed with the ship.

Banty had taken a night glass and went halfway up the shrouds. He reported when he came down, "She be the *Sting* sure enough, Captain."

"Good," Cooper said. He turned to his cox'n, "Quang, strike a spark for *SeaFire*."

"She's not far to larboard," Banty volunteered.

Johannes had apparently kept a good lookout's eyes on the ship as well. A spark was made and immediately one was returned. Within the turn of the glass, *SeaFire* was on station. They would ease up on the ship from both sides and strike.

"You may load the guns and swivels with grape," Cooper advised Spurlock.

The gunner nodded and then went to do as ordered. It was nearly two a.m. in the morning, and if the lookouts had been posted on *Sting*, they should have been spotted long ago.

"They may not have enough men to post lookouts," Dagan volunteered.

This made Cooper stop and think. If the ship had been taken by only a few men, he didn't want to needlessly kill the British seaman by a broadside. He looked at his watch, which read 2:15 a.m. He needed to signal Johannes, but how, especially at this hour. There was no way without possibly alerting the pirates. Johannes was a good captain. He'd see what Cooper was doing and hold his fire. If he didn't, more than a few were likely to die.

"Can we get another knot or two out of her?" Cooper asked the master.

"Aye, Captain, I expect that we can," the master replied.

T and Diamond spoke with the master. Soon, there were men called and set to squaring up the yards and tightening up the halyards. There was a noticeable increase that was felt right away. *Stag* was now a full ship's length ahead of *SeaFire*. They were almost up to the stern of *Sting*.

Boarders had gathered by the larboard rail. Men were at the swivels, and if the pirates presented to repel the boarders, the swivel loaded with grape would fire on the rogues. As the bowsprit eased passed the stern, a shout was heard on board *Sting*. Then there were several more shouts. Another minute and it would be too late. T quickly sent the forward boarders across, swinging down onto *Sting's* deck.

They rushed forward, screaming at the tops of their lungs. Only one man at the wheel gave fight and he was shot instantly. T led a group into the captain's cabin. Another rogue came on deck from below. Cooper pointed the man out and Jimmy Spurlin shot him. Shots were heard in the captain's cabin along with a flash of orange.

Two more men came up from below, but the man who had taken over the wheel shouted a warning, and they were both overrun and hacked down by *Stag's* boarders. T came on deck and gave the sign that all was secure.

The three ships hove to and lanterns were lit. The hatch cover over the forward hold was removed and British seamen came on deck.

Lieutenant Seymour reported to Cooper, "I wasn't sure that you'd understand my hint. But I'm certainly glad that you did."

Seymour explained that they had found the ten men adrift in a longboat. They had claimed to be seamen who had gotten away from the pirates, who'd taken their merchant ship. The night before last they'd managed to steal enough weapons, so they came on deck and killed the watch except for the midshipman.

Seymour continued, "They came to my cabin then, killing the marine sentry and waking me with a dagger at my throat. With me as their hostage, the rest of the crew did as they were told and were locked up in the hold at nightfall. It was just luck that we saw you. I convinced the leader that if we didn't close and hail, that you'd think it suspicious. Obviously, one of the rogues had been in the British Navy and agreed with me. Of course, none of them knew who the admiral was. I just hoped that you didn't think I was talking about your father-in-law."

It was nearly sunrise by now. Only two of the pirates were still alive, so Cooper sent *Sting* back to Antigua unescorted. He'd written a short report to the admiral and praised Lieutenant Seymour for using his wits as a means to seek help. He wasn't sure if it'd help but it wouldn't hurt. Having the lieutenant return in command of his ship without an escort would show confidence in the man as well.

CHAPTER THIRTY

D ROPPING ANCHOR AT SAVANNAH, Cooper turned the ship over to T. "Assign anchor watches but have the men return to the ship on Monday. As soon as you are satisfied with the ship's cleanliness, have Quang bring you to my house." Then as an afterthought, he told T to invite Kate. The family might want a peek at the woman their son had asked to be his wife.

Cooper took a ledger of the ships and prisoners that he'd captured, and gold, jewels, and coin that he'd taken and headed ashore with Dagan at his side. Cooper had been concerned about how the rigors of being at sea would affect Dagan, but in truth, the old salt looked better now than when they'd set sail. Was it the sea or was it feeling that he was a vital part of something again. Either way, Cooper was glad that Dagan had sailed with him, damn glad.

Eli was not at the warehouse office so Cooper gave his ledger to the company clerk. They'd make a tally of what should be coming to Cooper, his men and ships. The ledger was not one-hundred percent accurate. It was minus what Dagan and his cohorts had managed to confiscate before the official counts had been made. Cooper was sure that two of Dagan's cohorts were Banty and Spurlock. He'd seen the bulging pockets when they'd returned to the ship. He knew that they'd share with the 'old' crew so he'd said nothing.

Horses were being saddled for Cooper and Dagan when Suzanne Bledsoe was spied, so Cooper called to her.

"So Sir Pirate has made it home alive," Suzanne said.

Cooper smiled yet thought that Maddy needed to keep her mouth shut. It was a tight fit but he and Dagan managed to climb aboard the buggy. Suzanne wanted to know all the latest news. Had they rescued any damsels from being raped or put to death? This made Cooper and Dagan laugh. Suzanne would be shocked if she knew just how bad it had been for some of the women. Dagan set in on some tale that had the girl mesmerized.

They were at home finally, and Suzanne said, "I'll leave you to your homecoming," as Cooper and Dagan got down.

Cooper went in the back or kitchen door and was in the house before Maddy saw him. Rosa had exclaimed, "Bless Gawd."

Hearing Rosa, Maddy turned and rushed to Cooper. Her pregnant belly was sticking out so Cooper had to lean over to hug and kiss her.

"I'm fat as a cow," Maddy said.

"You're as pretty as a baby calf," Cooper said. He held her as close as he could and kissed her again.

Faith walked into the kitchen hearing the voices. Seeing Cooper, she called, "Gabe, Coop is home."

After greeting everyone, they all went to the table where Rosa set out the noon meal. Dagan, as if on cue, walked in, which resulted in more hugs and greetings. Once the meal was served, Dagan looked at Cooper and gave a slight nod. Gabe picked up on this right away. Too many years of his uncle being at his side let Gabe know that something was in the works.

Cooper chewed his meat, took a sip of his wine and spoke, "In a little while my first mate or first lieutenant, if you will, should arrive. He will have a beautiful woman with him. She is the widow of a surgeon, who was killed by pirates. She was one of the first prisoners that we rescued." He did not mention the abuse or rape that she had been subjected to. "Since we freed her, she has been acting as the surgeon for *Stag*. She has been a god-send. We rescued some children whose parents were murdered by the pirates. They witnessed a lot of things that I'd not want to mention in front of the ladies. Let's just say that it was things no one should see, especially children. Kate treated the children so that they felt comfortable talking to her and told her the whole horrible story of their ordeal."

"Who were their parents?" Faith asked.

"Sir Edward Westcoat and his wife," Cooper answered.

"Oh my, we know them," Faith said. "What brought them to the Caribbean?"

Gabe answered, "He was to have been the governor of one of the islands."

Cooper nodded and said, "I believe it was to be Grand Cayman, but I'm not sure." He paused and then said, "Kate, that's the lady's name. She is Jake's love." Now that he had everyone's attention, he continued, "Kathleen Timberlake is actually her name. She took the Westcoat children on board the flagship. Jake saw her and fell madly in love, so much so, that he's asked her to marry him. She didn't say no but she asked for time to think it over. I'm sure that her husband's murder is still fresh in her mind."

It was suddenly quiet in the room. Feeling the need to break the silence, Cooper said, "My mother dotes on her. She stayed with her and Jean Paul when we were at Antigua." This brought smiles and the conversation renewed.

General questions arose about the pirates and their success so far. Dagan answered most of the questions, for which Cooper was thankful.

"Are you through?" Maddy asked. "Through chasing those blackhearts."

Cooper gave a sigh, "No, we still have one to catch, Calico, the head man. So far, he has proven to be very elusive. We now have a clue as to where he might be. I need to talk with Eli, as his lair is near a place called Deadman Bay. Thus far, we've not found this on any of the charts we have. I figured if anyone would know where it is, it would be Eli."

"The need to talk to Eli was why you came home, not to see me," Maddy said, pouting.

"I used it as an excuse to come home to see you," Cooper countered.

"Good answer, Sir Pirate," Maddy said, leaning over to kiss her husband. Cooper flushed, causing Gabe and Faith to smile.

Later, the men stepped outside to smoke cigars. Normally, Cooper would have found an excuse to be alone with Maddy at this time, but he was expecting T and Kate at any time. Gabe was showing Cooper a wing off the house that they had started construction on.

"You would enter this room from the hall off the sitting room and it would also provide an easy access to the kitchen." Cooper was thinking *damn what a large addition for two people* when Gabe said, "We thought that you and Maddy's bedroom would be a bit small with a baby. This will be large enough for the bedroom and a nursery. Once the baby is large enough to have its own room, you will probably need to build a new house anyway."

Cooper nodded, thinking that he was glad he hadn't spoken his thoughts aloud. "Maddy and I have talked about building a house on the bluff up by the entrance to the drive. You can see out over the river from there. Maddy and I have sat on the bench there many times, watching the sunset."

The sound of a wagon interrupted the conversation. It was Quang driving T and Kate. Seeing Cooper, Quang drew up. "Captain Taylor say he see you tomorrow here."

Cooper nodded his head, "Did he say what time?"

"After coffee," Quang replied.

Cooper chuckled, that meant anytime before noon but probably mid-morning. T got down and Quang helped Kate down.

Cooper said, "T, Kate, this is Vice Admiral Sir Gabe Anthony, Maddy's father."

Gabe's eyes were glued on Kate, "My pleasure, Mrs. Timberlake." He seemed reluctant to release the woman's hand but finally did and shook T's hand.

"She has that effect on everyone," T quipped.

It was Gabe who flushed now. *No damn wonder Jake is stricken with this woman*, he thought. The group walked back to the house where Kate and T were introduced to Maddy and Faith.

Much later that night, when Maddy was getting out of her tub and Cooper had a towel drying her off, she said, "I wish that I was as pretty as Kate." .

"You are, dear, more so if you want to know the truth," Cooper responded.

"You are just saying that."

"No, Maddy, you are the most beautiful woman that I have ever seen." Cooper stared at his wife. Her belly looked big enough to pop and her breasts were so engorged that he was afraid to touch them.

"You just are going to stare?" Maddy asked.

"I don't want to hurt you."

"The only person who is going to get hurt is you, if you don't make mad love to me."

So he did.

CHAPTER THIRTY ONE

COOPER, T, JOHANNES, AND Virgil sat with Eli Taylor as he pointed out Deadman Bay. Eli said, using the stem of his pipe as a pointer, "It lies at the mouth of the Steinhatchee River."

The chart that Eli used had numerous hand drawings and notations that the captain had added in his years at sea. Being a pirate and always needing an escape route had caused Eli to make note of such places not documented on most charts. None of the flagship, *Minotaur's*, charts included Deadman Bay or any of Eli's other notations.

When Cooper mentioned this, Eli said, "They need to look at the old Spanish charts. Most of these places have been documented for years. There's a couple of fishing villages, Jena and Steinhatchee, which are located at the mouth of the river. The river starts out as fresh water but it turns brackish. The villages are isolated and are always on alert for Indian attacks. So they'll know when you arrive."

"What Indian tribes carry out the attacks?" T asked.

"Seminoles, I'd guess," Eli responded. "Indians and runaway slaves have migrated to the area after Jackson and his armies routed them out. Not all were Seminole, you understand, but the Seminoles have welcomed their Red brothers. Some of the blacks have even married into the tribe, becoming Black Seminole. Most of the men are welcomed because of their bravery."

The discussion about the Black Seminoles made Cooper think about Moses. He was half black and half Indian. The child was almost dead when Colonel Lee brought him home. He had been raised as a brother to Jonah Lee. The man was well respected and accepted. Something that was rare for the times.

"Is the river navigable?" Johannes asked.

Eli responded, "Not really, you can anchor in the mouth but to get up the river you have to use the ship's boats. I've made the trip a few times. We were attacked by Indians once, but we hugged the opposite shore and our muskets proved true driving them off. That was just before you joined us," Eli said to Johannes. "However, Banty, McKemie, Spurlock, and Diamond made the trip."

"They didn't seem to know where Deadman Bay was," Cooper threw out, wondering if they had held back the knowledge from him.

"I doubt any of them knew the name of the bay," Eli said. "Ask them if they know where the Steinhatchee River is, and I bet you'd get a different answer."

Cooper nodded, he could believe that. Back in the day, his pirates thought of booty, and the spirits and women it would gain them; not on maps, charts, or locations. That was what the captain and the quartermaster were for. There had been a change in the men since then...positive changes, good changes. Most of the men had saved some money since the change from pirate to privateer, and now pirate hunters.

When payment from the British government finally is paid for the ships that they'd taken, including one of the Navy's own frigates, plus their share of loot and merchandise on board the ships, each man would have a small fortune coming to him. T, as second in command of *Stag*, could buy a farm or a plantation if he wanted and never worry about returning to sea. But first the job had to be finished before the thoughts of the reward could materialize.

It suddenly came to Cooper, he had to do away with Calico, do away with the man. Yes, do away with him and his evil ways. He had to end this reign of torture, murder, and sexual abuse of children. The man was mentally deranged. A smart man alright, one who could organize but still a man who must be put to death. He'd not told the twins that Calico had taken Kathleen. He didn't want them to feel the same hurt and anxiety that he had. He could vividly recall the times that he, Jessie, Josie, and Kathleen had raised merry hell partying in London. No, he'd not tell the twins that would sadden them too much. He knew that he'd not rest until he'd freed his friend. If she was dead, well, he'd already decided what he was going to do to Calico. It would be one less to collect head money for. The men, his men, had not minded the ones that he'd let go so far. Maybe their thoughts were on their past. Coop had done what they hoped would have been done for any one of them had the table been reversed. No, they'd not minded…not minded at all.

✱✱✱

THE WOMEN HAD DECIDED that they wanted to be treated to a night out before the men sailed again. It might be the last time for Maddy before the baby came. Special reservations were made at the River Street Inn. The party would require most of the inn's seating capacity for James and Josie, Virgil and Jessie, Faith and Gabe, Cooper and Maddy. Jake Hex was with Suzanne Bledsoe and Dagan escorted Kate, and Eli was there with Debbie.

The inn had done a good job of making a circle of the tables, so that all in the group were close enough to join in on the conversations. Suzanne Bledsoe kept people laughing with her funny stories and wit.

James spoke at one point, "Kate, it's easy to see why my brother is smitten with you. But don't worry; we don't often gang up at inns or taverns in such a manner." Kate smiled but didn't respond. Thankfully, Suzanne quickly ended the uncomfortable silence with another hilarious tale.

Dagan placed his hand on Kate's and as he did so, she turned to him and he said, "For some there can only be one love. That's the way it was with me. However, it lasted until I was an old man. You loved your husband, but he was tragically taken. It's hard for you to turn loose. I know and understand that, but Kate, you are young, too young to spend your life trying to love a memory. I'm sure that your husband would be the first to tell you that. It's not often that real love comes to a person twice. If you love Jake, tell him. If you are worried about loving a man of the sea, talk to Faith or Maddy. They'll give you a true picture of what to expect. I don't mean to be hurtful or rude, Kate, but don't waste your life when you have a lifetime ahead of you."

Kate wiped a tear from her eye, leaned over and kissed Dagan on the cheek. "You sound like my father."

Dagan took a sip of his wine and set the glass down. He turned to Kate smiling, "I'm probably old enough to be your grandfather." He then added, "If I was a young man, none of these young blades would have a chance with you. But since I'm not, you'll have to settle for second best. Just make sure that the one you choose puts you on a pedestal and keeps you there."

Kate gripped his hand and smiling now, she said, "If you were just twenty years younger no one else would stand a chance."

They clinked their glasses together in a salute as Dagan responded, "You flatter an old man, but that was certainly nice."

Kate squeezed his hand again, "It was not meant to be just flattery. I meant every word of it."

The party lasted until Cooper noticed their server leaning against the corner wall, nodding his head. Eli took the check as everyone said goodnight.

Kate called to Faith, as they reached the carriages, "Would you mind us riding back together?" Dagan caught Kate's eye and gave her a wink and a nod.

Climbing in next to Dagan, Gabe spoke, "It seems that I've been supplanted."

"Aye, it does," Dagan responded. "What do you think of your future daughter-in-law?"

Gabe turned and looked at his uncle, "You think that she will marry Jake?"

"Aye, I'm too old. You are already taken, so who else is there?"

"Uncle, you never cease to amaze me," Gabe said.

❋ ❋ ❋

As COOPER AND MADDY lay down on the bed, they snuggled close. Maddy looked at Cooper and said, "When do you sail?"

"Tomorrow is Friday. Sailors are a superstitious lot and think it is bad luck to sail on Fridays. So I think we will sail on Saturday."

"Do you think that you'll be back before the baby is born?"

"Yes," Cooper said, and then added, "Dagan says that we will."

"Coop, will you be happy if it's a girl?"

"Yes, I will be happy whether it's a boy or a girl."

"I do want to give you a son, but I didn't want you to be dissatisfied if we had a daughter."

"Never would that happen, Maddy. The only thing is, if we have a daughter, she would be as beautiful as you are and I'd have to hire armed guards to keep watch over her. I'd probably send Quang to bring back six or eight of the most fearsome Chinamen to keep her beaus from trying to take her away from us."

Maddy kissed Cooper and then let her hand slide down low on her belly. "Like some rogue pirate?" she asked.

Cooper didn't answer. His mouth found Maddy's and he gave her a long passionate kiss. They didn't speak again for a long time. Then it was a simple, 'I love you', before sleep overtook them.

CHAPTER THIRTY TWO

IT WAS SIX BELLS of the morning watch. Cooper Cain walked over to *Stag's* sailing master, Gordon Brisco. Seeing Cooper, Brisco muttered, "Northwest by north, Captain."

Cooper nodded his head, wondering if the old master would be glad when *Stag* was back in the hands of the Royal Navy. They had rounded the Florida Keys during the night and were well on their way to Deadman Bay. Looking about the ship, he saw several of the crew eyeing him. Did they feel the tension that had mounted in him since setting sail? Even his old crew seemed to understand his mood and left him alone.

"Is it that obvious, T?" he asked.

"Aye, Captain. The men recognize the weight on your shoulders, and the need to put this business to an end, and the concern for the girl that Calico took, the one that you were friends with back in England. They'll be hard to hold back if she's been killed or mutilated."

"They'll have to get in line," Cooper hissed.

Dagan came on deck and crossed to the weather side where Cooper now stood. Most of the crew knew that Cooper was a hard riser and refrained from too much early morning chatter. This time, though, it was different. The captain was feeling remorseful. Dagan knew what was causing the effect on Cooper. He had told Cooper last night that he had a feeling, a premonition if you will, that they were going to be facing an old enemy.

Cooper looked at Dagan and whispered the name, "Phillip."

"You feel it as well," Dagan said.

"Yes. When Kathleen's father said the voice sounded familiar and Isabella described Calico as being somewhat deformed."

"You've hid it well," Dagan responded.

"I had to make sure in my mind. The dress of a dandy would fit Phillip. The ruthless nature is more than his usual, but if it is Phillip, the blast must have been too much. He was always proud of his features. I could picture him with any number of rich widows, making him their kept boy toy." Cooper took a deep breath and gave a sigh, "It's too bad that he chose the windward passage."

The wind had picked up since Cooper had come on deck. A wet sea mist was starting to dog the men on deck. T dismissed the hands not actually on watch.

"Shall we go down?" Cooper said to his friend. As he was stepping over the coaming to the companionway, he glanced back and saw Quang talking to one of Eli Taylor's men.

He was an odd sort. His name was Charlie Walking Bear. He was one of those men that were called a Black Seminole. He had sailed with Eli at times, and other times with Dominque Youx, and if he could be believed, he had sailed with José Gasper. He had said that Gasper had tired of trying to remember Walking Bear's name, so he named him Charlie. He was soon known as Charlie Walking Bear. The man was fluent in his native tongue. He might be a good man to have around if you had trouble with the Seminoles. Seeing the advantage of having such a man along, Cooper gladly accepted the offer. He carried a chest on board that was heavier than one man could carry. Without a word, Quang grabbed a handle and heaved the chest on a shoulder with ease. The two men had been together for the most part since then.

The minute that Charlie Walking Bear saw Kate, he asked, "Whose woman?"

It took a bit to explain that she wasn't anybody's woman; she was the ship's doctor. After a bit of back and forth, it came out she was a medicine woman. Charlie Walking Bear's Indian instinct took over and he gave a few bows as he backed away. He said nothing further about Kate.

Once in the cabin, Josiah was quick to serve a cup of coffee with a tot of brandy. Dagan tasted the brew, which immediately brought back memories of Gabe's brother, Vice Admiral Lord Gilbert Anthony's cabin servant, Silas. At the time, he was known as having the best coffee in the fleet. Others had tried to imitate his brew, but never could get the recipe exact. Josiah's blend was close, but not exact. Poor old Silas had passed on. When Lord Anthony hauled down his flag, Silas had bought a small inn. He'd spent the rest of his days tending the bar and telling sea stories as his daughter ran the place. He had named the place 'The Admiral's Pantry.' Times like this made Dagan a bit melancholy. He often wondered why he'd been spared so long, but he put that out of his mind. It did no good to question God's plan.

✹✹✹

IT WAS PAST THE noon hour when excited voices could be heard on deck. Dagan had left to go topside and Cooper found himself thinking on Calico or Phillip if he was indeed the pirate leader. Cooper ,putting his thoughts aside, almost collided with Midshipman Shirreffs.

"My apologies, Captain. Indians have been sighted." The middy, making room for his captain, followed Cooper on deck.

On the starboard side, several Indians could be seen in canoes just off the shore. Charlie Walking Bear shouted out a greeting. Some of the Indians waved, but didn't make a move toward the ship.

"They headed to village after fishing." Charlie Walking Bear said. "There will be lots of full bellies tonight."

"I didn't expect to see Indians this soon," T said.

The master responded, "We've had a fresh wind since rounding the Keys. If Captain Taylor's charts are right, we should reach Deadman Bay tomorrow afternoon."

Dagan heard the words but he already knew it. He could feel it. One way or another, the end was near. The end for Calico... but who else might fall?

As the sun set and men gathered on deck, Leon, the fiddler, came on deck. Cooper had picked Leon up as a boy in New Orleans. He had to be in his teens now. He did very little on board the ship other than carry messages on occasion. At night, though, he'd pick up his fiddle and entertain the men dancing about and playing his fiddle. He, at times, would play a slow, sorrowful tune but most of the time he sawed out one shanty after another. He'd just finished one that had Charlie Walking Bear dancing. Now he sat down and played a slow, sad one.

Listening to Leon, Cooper spoke to Dagan, "A fiddler was playing a mournful tune when we met, Dagan."

"Aye, Old Gooley. The boy's not lived long enough to have faced the hardships and hurt to really bring out the soulfulness in his play. But if he lives, he will."

"Think he'll sell his soul of the fiddler's green?" Cooper asked.

Dagan smiled, "I doubt if he's old enough to have heard that tale yet."

It wasn't long before men were yawning, so Leon put up his fiddle and the men drifted down to their hammocks. A few of the men finished up a cigar or their pipe.

Charlie Walking Bear had the stub of a pipe in his mouth when he approached Cooper, "Cap'n, bring fiddle boy if he come; he music boy. Seminole like. Bring him and medicine woman too. May have need for big medicine when we go."

Cooper shook his head, not actually agreeing but letting the man know that he understood.

Kate walked up as Charlie Walking Bear turned away. "That made it easy."

"What?"

"The Indian said that I'd be needed. I was going to ask to come, but now as our guide feels that I'll be needed, there shouldn't be any discussion."

Cooper stood there staring at Kate. She was as bad as Maddy in finding reasons to have her way. Did all women possess this trait? He looked up. T and Dagan were both smiling.

"Well, damme!" he exclaimed.

CHAPTER THIRTY THREE

THE CREW HAD BEEN called to shorten sail in preparation for anchoring. The winds had been steady. *Stag* and *SeaFire* had made good time. Cooper had just come down to his cabin to dress. He would wear his best uniform. Quang passed him his jacket. Looking in the mirror, Cooper recalled a fellow in New Orleans who cut a dashing figure as he made to go meet his opponent. "You are dressed very fashionably," his second had said. "Yes," the man replied. "I intend to woo a young lady if I win and if not, I want to be the best dressed corpse in New Orleans."

Above, the voice of T and Diamond, the bosun rang out above all others. "Haul taut...that's it me lads.

"Helm a-lee." That was T. It was amazing that T, somewhat short of stature, could bellow like a man ten feet tall.

"Let go the anchor!" It was Diamond again.

The ship had a good crew, top seamen and top fighters. Looking out the stern, Cooper caught a glimpse of Johannes Ewers putting his ship through the same maneuvers as *Stag*.

"Are the men ready?" Cooper asked Quang.

The Chinaman nodded as he handed Cooper his hat. "Men ready, boat ready." Quang would never make it as a spit and polish British cox'n. Especially an admiral's cox'n, like Jake Hex, but Cooper wouldn't trade him for the world.

A thought came to Cooper. He remembered when he first met Bart. He wasn't high in spit and polish either, but lieutenants jumped when he growled, as did a few of the younger captains.

What was it the tavern keeper had said, "I'd sooner kiss a cobra than anger Bart. A sure way of doing that is to cross Lord Anthony." Cooper had seen Quang in action. He was a fierce warrior as well.

"Time to go up," Coop said to Quang.

Josiah stepped out of the pantry, "Have a care, sir."

Cooper stretched out his arm and shook Josiah's hand. "If I should fall, you know that you will have a home at Thunderbolt."

"Aye," Josiah replied, and then turned his head so that Cooper wouldn't see the tears that poured down his cheeks.

Stepping out of the companionway onto the deck, the first people that Cooper saw was Dagan and Kate. At dawn that morning, when Cooper had come on deck, Kate was there and dressed almost like a man.

"I don't mean to be inappropriate or improper, Kate, but when we go ashore today, I want you to dress in such a way as… so that any person can pick you out as a woman from a good distance," Cooper said.

Kate smiled, "Your flushing, Captain. Do I take it to mean that you want my wares accented…much as they were when I asked to join the ship?"

Cooper remembered the sharp outline of Kate's breasts, the brown of her nipple just visible in the seaman slops. "Perhaps not that noticeable," he said, still smiling at the image in his mind. "But close." *I need the men alert for danger*, he thought, *not having their eyes glued on Kate's wares.*

Two ship's boats were being hoisted over the side. As men went over the side, muskets were handed down to them. There were bags of powder and shot draped across his men's shoulders. In their belts were knives and tomahawks. Swivel guns were mounted in the bow of each boat along with a small keg of powder and bags of grape shot. A boat pulled up alongside *Stag*. It was Johannes Ewers from *SeaFire*.

He grabbed Cooper's hand, "I wish that I was going with you."

Cooper smiled, "Aye, but I need someone to take the ships back if I fall."

"T can do it," Johannes countered.

"Aye, but Maddy knows you," Cooper responded.

Johannes nodded his head, "I promise you this, Coop. Nothing will go up or come down the river that I don't blast to eternity, if you don't return."

"I'm confident of that, old friend," Cooper said.

The boats were loaded when Cooper went down the battens. Charlie Walking Bear was in the bow of the first boat. Ox sat next to him, ready to fire the swivel if hostiles appeared and Charlie Walking Bear's words didn't prevent the Seminoles from attacking. Quang had the tiller. Dagan and Kate sat just in front of Cooper and Quang.

T was in charge of the second boat, and Banty had the tiller. Spurlock was in the bow to man the swivel if necessary and the backwoodsman sharpshooter, Spurlin, sat next to him.

Two villages, one on each side of the river were in plain view of Deadman Bay. Men had gathered on one side of the river bank. One man stepped out as the boats closed with the bank and pulled the boat's bow up on the shore. Ox jumped out and tugged it further onto the shore. Cooper got out of the boat, and it didn't take long to realize that the eyes of the men gathered on shore were focused on Kate. Hopefully, any hostiles would do the same thing.

"I'm Cooper Cain," Coop said to the group. "Who is in charge here?"

"That galoot with his eyes wide and his mouth hanging open," someone said.

The group had the appearance of fishermen. Several boats were on the bank and Cooper could see several fishing nets stretched.

One of the men punched their leader, "Close your mouth before the green flies fill it."

"I'm Tobias Tatum," the man said. "This be Barney Smith and the other fellow is James Wayne."

"I've been given a commission by both our country, and England to purge the seas of pirates," Coop said.

Barney snickered, "None of us be pirates."

Cooper smiled, "I'm sure that you're not. However, we've gotten information linking the pirate leader to this area. A man called Calico. He dresses in clothes such as a dandy might wear and we hear he may be deformed."

The three men looked at each other. Finally, Tobias cleared his throat and spat. "There's a man who passes this way time and again. Never stops and never speaks. He comes in a ship and usually heads up river after dark. He has had Indians with him on occasion when he comes back down. He's up above the falls, and has a camp set up, just north of there."

"Tell me about the falls," Cooper asked.

"It ain't much in the general tradition of waterfalls. It's actually where a limestone shelf crosses the river. Depending on the tide and rain, the depth is likely to change. I've ridden my horse over it. If you are paddling upstream, you'll have to carry your boats above the falls to put them back in upstream. The water in the river up there is fresh. It's brackish here."

"What is the land like in that area?" Cooper inquired.

"It's a swamp when it rains; other times its low or bottom-land. Lots of pine and hardwood trees."

"There are all kinds of critters," Barney cut in. "Wild hogs, snakes, some gators, and every other creature that lives in the woods. If you're going after that dandy, I'd leave the boats at the falls and go the rest of the way on foot."

"How far is it from here?" Cooper asked.

"It is eight miles to the falls and maybe another mile to the dandy's camp." Looking at Kate again, Tobias then gazed up at the sun. "You should spend the night here and start out fresh in the morning."

"We'd like to get close before he knows that we're here," Cooper said.

"They knew that you were here an hour ago," Tobias said. "The Seminoles keep a lookout for him, for which he brings gifts, even women to them."

Dagan and Cooper looked at one another. The river men picked up on it right away.

"He got one of your women?"

"You might say that," Cooper said.

"If the Seminoles have her already you better have something mighty valuable to trade. Those men you got aren't enough to deal with a hunting party, let alone a war party."

"Calico will consider this woman special. I doubt that he'd give or trade her away."

"I hope that you are right, mister," one of the river men said.

"Captain," Spurlock corrected, "He isn't a mister, he's a captain."

"That's alright," Cooper said. "I'm sure that he's not used to the ways of the sea." Cooper didn't want to antagonize these men. They might or might not be in league with Calico.

Charlie Walking Bear pushed to the front of the men, "We go on to falls now."

Cooper wasn't sure why the guide said what he did, but Cooper was inclined to trust his judgment.

"It'd be easier to camp here," Tobias called out, as the men loaded back into the boat.

Once they were upstream, Charlie Walking Bear spoke again, "Men at camp, good men. They think only of women, but good men. Me see two men run off up river. They not good men, they go warn bad man. Let me and that man," Charlie was pointing at Spurlin, "out here. We catch bad men, they not run. We meet at falls."

They pulled over to the bank that Charlie Walking Bear pointed too, and he and Spurlin got out. "Meet at falls," he said, and with that the two men bounded out of sight.

They reached the falls just before dark. It had been a tough pull going against the flow of the river. Cooper wondered if they should have brought along a sail.

T spoke to Cooper, as the men pulled the boats up, "I'd feel more comfortable if we kept a watch up."

"Aye, I'm no hand at fighting the Seminoles, but I'd like to be at least halfway prepared," Cooper replied.

"A fire, Captain?" This was from Spurlock.

"A small one," Cooper said. "We'll arrange the boats so that they'll offer a bit of cover and also shield the fire some."

T had the camp set up and then issued the men a tot of rum. Kate walked to the river to wet a handkerchief and wiped her face and neck. A cry escaped her and she jumped back. Cooper ran to her, a small torch in his hand.

"There," she pointed. "It was a snake, a thick black snake. He opened his mouth and it was white," Kate cried.

"A cottonmouth," Banty said. "We saw them all the time in the swamps between Barataria and New Orleans. Be glad that it opened its mouth. They do that before they bite. If you see the cottonmouth, you can usually get back like you did. I know a lot of fellows that got bit, and most of them died." He took Kate's handkerchief and stepped into the water. He wet it and squeezed the excess out, handing it back to Kate. He smiled then and went back to camp.

❊❊❊

IT WAS GROWING LATE, and Cooper and Dagan still sat by the fire. Kate, in spite of her declaration that she'd not sleep on the ground with snakes around, was wrapped in a blanket near the fire snoring slightly.

Cooper was trying to keep awake until Charlie Walking Bear and Spurlin returned. Dagan had entertained him with tales of Maddy when she was a small child. One minute all was well and then Charlie and Spurlin emerged.

"Men no talk," Charlie Walking Bear said.

Spurlin's tomahawk had a dark stain on its handle. "It took a while to get rid of the bodies and then we scouted Calico's camp since we were so close. You have to be careful, Captain. The man has snakes hanging on ropes from tree limbs."

CHAPTER THIRTY FOUR

EVERYONE WAS AWAKE BY dawn, even Cooper. He had not slept well, worrying one minute about Kathleen Woodham, his old friend from England; and then worrying about Maddy and the baby. He'd slept finally but not a restful sleep.

Kate walked to the river with Dagan beside her. A slight chill filled the air. Vapors rose from the water, as it was warmer than the morning air. A blue heron made a loud racket, having been startled by the people coming down to the river. The flapping of his wings seemed to cause other waterfowl to rise up in flight. Dagan couldn't remember so many birds at once, and they were different species. He identified an egret, a cormorant, and an ibis in addition to the heron.

"The forest is alive this morning," he said, and then gripped Kate's arm. He'd gotten a glimpse of an Indian darting behind a large pine tree. "Wet your cloth and come with me," he said in a low voice. He was armed, but what would one pistol do?

Kate recognized the change in Dagan and she did as he bid. Walking back to the camp she hissed, "I think that I'll just stay away from the damn river." Dagan couldn't help but smile.

The camp was in sight of the river. As they got around a tree, Dagan and Kate could see that the men had all gathered around the fire and voices could be heard. Charlie Walking Bear was talking to some Indians. They spoke in a different tongue. Charlie Walking Bear had said that the Seminoles spoke Creek and Mikasuki. While Dagan couldn't understand the language, their words didn't appear to have any hostility in the conversation or hand movements.

Dagan let Kate walk to the group in front of him. The Indian talking with Charlie suddenly stopped. He smiled and pointed at Kate and spoke excitedly. Charlie shook his head and made some gestures. He then turned to Kate, bowed and held out his hand.

Kate instinctively took the offered hand and stepped forward. There was more speech and gesturing, and then mumbling was heard. The Seminoles bowed and then backed out.

Charlie Walking Bear spoke, as soon as the Seminoles were out of sight. "The chief told us that strange man with big medicine not far. I told the chief that he had your woman," indicating Cooper. "He saw Kate and wanted to buy her. I told him she was no man's woman, she was a medicine woman. I told him a man could be shot and she could reach inside him and take out the ball and hold it in her fingers. This awed them and he apologized for wanting to buy her as no one could buy a medicine woman. He said that if we were to get Cooper's woman back, her medicine had to be bigger than the green man. He finally said that the green man could put a snake's mouth to his heart and it couldn't bite him."

"He must have skin of leather," Banty volunteered.

"I saw a preacher in New Orleans play with snakes. He had a breast plate on," Ox interrupted. "I bumped him once and he clinked. Don't forget he's got snakes hanging on tree limbs along the path."

"Damme," T exclaimed. "I'm tired of all this snake talk."

The men finished their meal and swallowed down their coffee. They set out then, following behind Charlie Walking Bear and Jimmy Spurlin. The path was slow and winding.

"Don't step over a log or downfall without looking over the other side," Spurlin cautioned. "Snakes like to lie close to them and can bite you as you step over. Look even if someone has just gone over the log."

The early morning chill had dissipated as the sun came up. Perspiration was now starting to bead up and run down the group's faces and neck. Cooper had long since removed his uniform coat and slung it over his shoulder. Mosquitoes began to swarm and bite as it warmed up. It was then that the smell of smoke caught Cooper's attention. Dagan and T stepped up.

"Eucalyptus," Dagan questioned.

Spurlin walked back to where Cooper was. "What's that smell?" Cooper asked him.

"Gum…or some call it ecualyptus."

"Sweet gum?" Ox asked.

"No, a different gum," Spurlin replied.

Spurlin seemed in a hurry, so they continued on. They'd not walked another five minutes when they came up with Charlie Walking Bear. Kate had to put her hand to her mouth to choke off a loud gasp. There along the trail, writhing snakes hung from ropes tied to tree limbs. The sight was horrifying.

"Watch this," Spurlin said. He took a long pole that he and Charlie Walking Bear had cut. He pushed the snake from side to side…nothing. But when he lifted the snake, taking the weight off the rope, a board jumped up from the ground. Spikes were driven thru it.

"That would make you a dead man fast," Charlie said.

"If it didn't, it would make you jump back and get a set of fangs in you," Spurlin added.

"Still a dead man," Charlie repeated.

"What do we do?" Cooper asked.

"We'll see if the same thing happens on this side. If it does, you walk in my steps or go back."

Cooper swallowed hard and said, "Everyone pick up a stick. If a snake swings near you, use the stick to block it, but don't swing hard. We don't want it swinging back on you."

It took fifteen to twenty minutes to walk the trail, past the snakes. The area then opened up. Charlie had a long stick testing the ground, and then a large snap was heard. A bear trap, and it had been camouflaged well.

"Whew," someone breathed.

"It's probably clear, but everyone continues to step in our footprints," Spurlin said.

They had gone but a few feet before Charlie Walking Bear stopped again. The ground looked as normal as the rest of it but when Charlie poked it, it seemed soft. He stepped back and motioned to a partially decayed limb on the trail. Rolling it cautiously, and looking out for snakes, he and Quang picked it up and walked back to where he'd left the pole. Together the two men swung it back and forth and on the third swing they let it go. It landed a few feet out from the pole. It hit the ground with a thud and then crashed down into a pit about head high.

Someone in the party said, "Much more of this and I'll die of fright."

"No more," Charlie Walking Bear said.

A sandy trail was in front of them and was full of fresh footprints.

"They came in from the west, so we'll go back that way," Spurlin said.

CHAPTER THIRTY FIVE

AN INDIAN STOOD ABOUT twenty to thirty yards up the trail. A horse and two wheeled cart was behind him. A man and youth were sitting in the cart. The man was dressed in green.

"Congratulations, Cooper Cain, you put it all together. Once I took that pathetic British frigate, I knew you would. I started to lead you straight here but then I thought 'why?' Let my men play with him first. Come on, Cooper, I have an old friend of yours here. She's not so snobby, as she once was…nor as pretty. The insects play hell with a woman's sensitive skin."

"You harm her and you'll regret it," Cooper shouted.

"Regret it? Don't flatter yourself, cousin. What could you possibly do to me that you haven't already done?" Cooper didn't speak for a moment. "Didn't you recognize me, Cooper? I was sure that you would have figured it all out by now. So you see, cousin, I couldn't get to your wife or those slutty twins, but Kathleen. Our dear Kate, as we called her, always throwing her wares at us, but never letting us taste the fruit. It was she that made me hate women. I'm sure, though, that you tasted the forbidden fruit."

"No, Phillip, I never did. It drove me crazy a few times, but I never tasted the fruit as you say, neither with Kate nor with the twins. "

Phillip sounded sad suddenly, "I always thought you did, Coop. I'm sorry I didn't believe you when you said that you hadn't."

"Why didn't you seek other women, Phillip? The widow Raines begged you to top her."

"I couldn't. She smelled of sickened perfume and breathed so heavy, I almost ran from her chamber."

"What about Lydia Dykes? She wanted you, I know," Cooper said.

"Lydia? Didn't you know, Cooper, that Lydia was a man?"

Cooper and his group had continued to walk forward. He was now almost at the cart.

"No closer," the boy with Phillip snarled. He held up his hands and moved his fingers back and forth, showing off the blades attached to his fingers.

"Don't come any closer, cousin. Charles gets very jealous," Phillip said.

Cooper spit, causing Charles to snarl.

"It's alright, Charles, we are just having a family discussion." Without a pause, Phillip returned to his conversation like it had never been interrupted. "Yes, cousin, Lydia was a man. He took me to a place at the Gardens where I had the most gratification I'd ever had. You don't know what we did, Cooper. We had sex while sacrificing a nun. It was a whore really, but she was dressed like a nun. We gave her a drink that was drugged so that she didn't feel anything. I got to sacrifice her, as I was the newest person in the group."

"Santa Maria," Charlie Walking Bear whispered.

He must have gotten that from Gasper, Cooper thought.

"It's a feeling you never reach again," Phillip said.

"Dreadful, just dreadful," Cooper said.

"Yes, and now you've come to put an end to it, cousin. Yes, we have had our family talk but now let's get back to why you are here. It is such a distasteful thought. If you care to look around, cousin, you will see my black Seminoles have surrounded your group. One word from me and you will all die."

"Jimmy!" Coop called to Spurlin, the backwoodsman. "If it's the last thing that you do, put a bullet through Charles's head. Quang, if he fails you finish it."

"Him die," Quang said.

Phillip suddenly realized that he could win, but he would lose what was dearest to him. Charles started to move.

"Stop," Cooper shouted. "One more step and you'll die."

It was a standoff. Cooper took another step to separate himself from the group, but Dagan took a step with him.

"Stay back," Cooper whispered.

"Not today," Dagan replied.

"I'll offer you a way out, Phillip, a duel. You win and you are left unharmed, but Kathleen goes with us. If I win, you give yourself up. I'll plead for jail and not the gallows."

"Oh, how thoughtful you are but, as you can see, you've already left me incapable of accepting your offer."

"Your champion then, I know that you have one," Cooper replied.

Phillip smiled, "Would you fight a woman, Cooper? She is not your average woman with large catheads and little round arse. A warrior of a woman she is, who has never lost or shied away from battle."

"I will."

Charlie Walking Bear took a step up and said, "She is a murderess. She's from the Gullahs. They say that she is a witch woman who has taken an enemy's heart from his chest while he was still breathing. She dips her blades in the venom of snakes. If you are cut, you will die whether she dies or not."

Phillip spoke to the Indian holding the horse's head. He then looked at Cooper and said, "Would you care for a cup of tea while we wait? This heat is so depressing. Charles will get it for us."

"He stays," Cooper said.

"Not feeling social today, cousin. I guess that we will endure the heat," Phillip replied.

Cooper was close enough to see through the veil, and Phillip was indeed deformed. His ear on this side was missing, and also his eyebrow. The skin was thickened and scarred. His neck was webbed so he could only turn it so far as he moved his body. A white mitten-like glove fit the one hand and he only had a thumb and finger on the other hand. Phillip's shoes, what Cooper could see of them, were overly large and he had stained dressings under his stockings.

"Don't let his appearance make you lose sight of why you are here, Cooper. If you feel sorry for the man, you give the son of Satan the advantage," Dagan said.

"I understand," Cooper replied.

A shout of 'Seba' was heard and taken up by the Indians as she walked through the crowd. As she came to where Phillip's cart and Cooper's group were, she stopped and crossed her hands. She didn't wear a top but was covered below with a pair of new britches. Her chest was flat with only small mounds and nipples for breasts. She was well muscled for a woman. She wore a belt and hanging from it was a small sword with a gold handle. A tomahawk handle was tucked inside the belt also. But what appeared strange was what looked like chicken or rooster feet. The legs were wrapped in different color dyed leather strings. The claws were yellow but the spurs were painted yellow also.

"Those are poisoned," Charlie Walking Bear said when he saw where Cooper was gazing.

Phillip gave the warrior woman a bow with his head. "Thank you for coming, great Seba. This man would challenge me. He is the reason for my physical appearance. If you beat him, I will give you his woman as a slave."

Cooper was not sure which woman Phillip meant. "That was not the bargain," Cooper said.

"That's my bargain," Phillip countered.

"Quang," Cooper called. "Win or lose, kill Charles."

Phillip went to speak but Cooper held up his hand. "That's my bargain, Phillip. Now show me Kathleen."

"Why not," Phillip said, speaking to the Indian.

Cooper spoke loudly as the Indian started off, "Wait. Ox!"

"Aye, Cap'n."

"Go with him, but watch closely."

The big brute nodded and sidled up to the Indian. They returned before too long. Kathleen was emaciated, and her delicate skin was red and welted, from top to bottom. She had numerous cuts on her breasts, abdomen, and the inner part of her thighs. None of the cuts were deep though, just deep enough to hurt. The insect bites looked worse. Her eyes were swollen almost shut. Her lips were swollen and cracked. Her fingers were also swollen, and they looked like small sausages. She was filthy as well.

"How could you, Phillip?" Cooper asked.

The man took a breath and gave a sigh. "I must admit, it was Charles. He does like to play and it's not within me to tell him no."

"Kill Charles," Cooper said.

"No," Phillip shouted.

"A trade then, you send me Kathleen and I'll let Charles live."

Ox, without being told to, picked up the woman and started walking to Cooper. Charles jumped forward and with the blade on his index finger, he ripped a long cut down Kathleen's back. It turned crimson immediately.

"You little sodomite," Ox shouted and kicked the boy in the stomach and chest before walking over to his group. He laid her on the coat that Cooper handed him and Kate came to her with her medical bag.

CHAPTER THIRTY SIX

SINCE I WAS THE one challenged, we choose the weapons," Phillip called out. "It will not surprise you, cousin, that we are choosing blades. I think though, that our training with Jean Paul won't be of much help with Seba's type of play." He then hung his head down, "It is a pity that I never learned the truth about you and Kathleen until today. I think that your death will rest heavy on my shoulders."

Cooper could feel, once again, his heart changing. Dagan did not want his friend's mind clouded by sympathy for a man who had done so much evil.

Dagan looked at Phillip and said, "Will that knowledge make you change your ways? Are you ready to admit your mistakes and surrender? Are you ready to face a judge and be tried for your misdeeds?"

Phillip stamped the floor of his cart with a cane. "Heavens no, man. I enjoyed every moment. Watching pathetic people beg for their life. I was like a god. I held control over life and death."

Dagan smiled, "I'm sure that you'll remember that as you smell the sulfur and burn in hell."

"You forget," Phillip shouted out, "I've been through the fires of hell and lived." He gave an eerie laugh as he said what he did.

"No, you've not tasted hell in its fullest, not even ten seconds of it. You were in a hellish explosion, true enough. I was there, remember? Now look at what ten seconds of hell on earth did to you. That's just a taste of what you'll feel when you spend eternity in the pits."

"Enough...enough," Phillip screamed. "Let the combat begin."

As Cooper walked over to shed his shirt and pick his weapons, Dagan walked to Seba. He spoke to the warrior woman for a few minutes. When he left her, Seba's eyes were wide and she nervously gripped and released the grip on her sword.

Cooper approached Seba with a good blade and tomahawk in his hand. As he did so, he saluted her with his blade. Seba gave a bow in return. He found himself ill-prepared as Seba began to circle, waving her hands up and down as she circled backwards. They made a complete circle of this, then two, and then three as Cooper stood still other than pivoting so as to keep her facing him.

It was on the seventh circle that she struck. It was only his years of training under Jean Paul that saved him. When she lunged most people would have tried to jump back. Had he done that, Seba's blade would have plunged into his chest. Instead, he side-stepped her approach.

When he did so, Seba was off balance and fell forward. Cooper's blade lashed out, cutting Seba's upper arm deeply. As the blade slipped off her arm, it caught the side of her upper back slicing into it for about a three inch cut. It was not deep, but deep enough so that the loss of blood from her upper arm and back would weaken her. Blood would drain down her arm and make the handle of her blade slick and hard to hold.

Seba backed away and paused. She did not look at her wound. She watched Cooper, and when he didn't move she started the waving and backing around again, only in the opposite direction this time. She'd only gone one turn this time when she lunged.

This time Cooper ducked down and parried her lunge. Had he side-stepped, she would have severed his head. He heard the whoosh as the blade barely passed above his head. When he parried, his blade hit the handle and now she bled from a puncture below her thumb.

Seba's eyes widened as she back away. *Was he an angel of death as the old man had said? Was the scar across his face really from a battle with the devil?* She'd never missed twice and after two of her favorite moves, she hadn't drawn blood. In the past, she'd taken men's hearts with her blades by now. The old man had said she would be granted mercy if she threw down her weapons. They only wanted the evil warlock. Her mind was running away with her. But, she was Seba, the warrior. If she threw down her blade who would she be? Who would bow to her then? Who would hold her high as a lioness—nobody. She'd lived as a warrior. If the Gods called for it, she would die a warrior. She would not call for mercy. She would die as a warrior should—with honor.

The blonde haired man with the hideous scar had fought fairly, so far. He could have hurt her much worse had he pressed his advantage when he had it. It was almost like he was playing with her. She held up her blade, a sign to wait. She took the cock's claws from her belt and tossed them aside. She would not use the cock's claws dipped in venom on an honorable adversary.

Phillip watched with dismay. He'd seen Seba rake a man over some insult and watched him die. That was what he wanted her to do to Cooper, to rake him. He wanted to see him die from the venom. He wanted to see him suffer.

When Seba had thrown the cock's claws aside, she picked up her blade, pointed at Cooper and attacked. She was especially good for an untrained person who had nothing but raw talent. It was little wonder that she had won and by winning, she had struck fear in those who watched her. She attacked with vigor, but it was soon evident that her strength was ebbing with the blood loss. She charged with all she had. The clank and ring of steel on steel filled the air.

Cooper had defended her thrusts but had not attacked. He did so now with his blade a blur, pushing her back, back and further back. Then with a twist of his wrist he took her blade, sending it in the air and kicking out with his boot. He caught the blade out of the air and looked down where she lay on the ground. He stuck the point of his blade in the dirt. He then took her blade in both hands and held it to his forehead. He then surprised everyone as he knelt beside her as she lay on her back and returned the weapon to her. A murmur rose up from the Indians gathered around.

Everyone had been watching the duel and didn't see Charles pick up the poisoned cock's claws. He ran toward Cooper, who had turned to retrieve his blade. Pausing to rake Seba with the claws, he raced toward Cooper as someone shouted a warning. Cooper, without thinking, spun with his blade in hand. The sickening sound of the blade slicing through flesh was heard as Charles' head was severed from his body and fell thudding to the ground.

Phillip screamed as severed arteries pumped spurts of blood from the headless torso. He lifted a stick and was aiming at Cooper when Dagan fired his pistol. The stick was a disguised weapon. When Phillip had raised and pointed it at Cooper, Dagan had acted instinctively and quickly. The ball entered the side of Phillip's head.

Phillip, the pirate leader known and feared as Calico, was dead. His brutality had ended with a pistol ball. The words 'Calico' and 'Axel the Ax' would no longer be a threat. In time, the threat of pirates would rise again. It always did, but for now, it was over.

❋ ❋ ❋

THEY MADE A SEARCH of Phillip's compound and found three more young girls, nude, their bodies lined by cuts from Charles' little finger blades and welts and knots in their skin from insect bites.

Money was also found in the compound. The coins were from many nations, a testament as to how wide Phillip's pirates struck. A cage with rats sat by a wooden box filled with various snakes — cottonmouths, rattlesnakes, and copperheads. *The Indians could do as they wished with the snakes,* Cooper thought.

Phillip's house they found full of pictures and drawings of torture machines and devices used throughout the ages.

Seeing these, T said, "The man had a hunger for torture, didn't he?"

"His soul was tortured," Dagan said. "He was filled with jealousy and thought people ridiculed him behind his back."

Kate brought Kathleen into the house and bathed her. She treated her wounds with a salve and she was given food and a small glass of wine. Cooper went in to see her. She lay on her stomach with a sheet over her.

"You came and got me," the woman whispered.

"Yes, I came to get you and stop Phillip," Cooper replied.

"He said that you would. He also said that you'd not rest until you had my body again. I told him that we'd come close but never did we go all the way," Kathleen said.

"I told him the same thing," Cooper said.

"You can have me, Cooper. As dreadful as I may look, you can take me for all the times I led you on. Take me and do with me as you will."

"No, Kathleen, I am a married man with a child on the way."

Tears came to Kathleen's eyes, "I caused this didn't I, Coop? My flirting caused this all."

224

"No, you raised some humors but I didn't act like Phillip. Others that you flirted with went on with their lives. Phillip didn't turn out like he did because of you."

"I offered myself to you so that you could treat me badly if you wanted to. You could do anything that you desire to; as I feel that I must be punished."

"You do not need to be punished. You've already gone through more than you deserve to."

"He killed my husband and maybe my father," Kathleen said.

Cooper replied, "It was your father who told me that Phillip had you."

Kathleen turned and reached out her arms. "You saved my father."

"Yes, or we did."

"Thank you, still my husband is gone. They made him watch as they violated me and then when he tried to help me they killed him. When Phillip saw me, he didn't let the men have me anymore, only the boy with the knives. He liked to cut you and make you bleed."

"He's dead now also, Kathleen. You've nothing to fear now. You're safe," Cooper said, and she finally slept.

"She's sure been through a lot. I gave her something to help her rest. With rest and proper care she will recover physically. Mentally may take a while," Kate said.

"She's feeling so guilty that she offered herself to me," Cooper said.

Kate nodded, "I heard. I was at the door."

"Spying on me?"

"No, Coop, I was just ready to help if you needed it. But you are right, Calico made her think that all of his misdeeds were because of her. It will take time to get over that."

Cooper replied, "I wonder if being around Jesse and Josie would help."

"It wouldn't hurt. Now, let's leave and let her rest."

CHAPTER THIRTY SEVEN

THE TRIP BACK TO Savannah and home was uneventful. Everyone wanted to hear about the capture of Calico. When they learned who Calico actually was, Maddy said, "I'm glad that it was Dagan who shot him. As bad as he was, at least you won't be dealing with the knowledge that you killed your own cousin."

Kathleen was up and about fairly soon and outwardly seemed to be almost her old self. Being with Jessie had helped her. Word was sent by ship to her father that she was safe. When the ship returned to Savannah, Merriweather was on it. He wanted to see his daughter.

"She's the only family I have now," Merriweather said. "My milksop of a son was surprised to see me back. He said that he didn't think the damnable pirates would keep their word so he didn't send the ransom." Seeing the look of disbelief on his young friend's face, Merriweather said, "Oh yes, damn him." The old gentleman continued, "A lady was taken and her husband treated her badly. He even encouraged the pirates to have their way with her. He was recently found dead behind a brothel. Good riddance, I'd say. Well, this lady and I have struck up an acquaintance and though I'm a few years her senior, we certainly enjoy each others' company."

"I wish you well," Cooper responded. He didn't want to tell Kathleen's dad it was suspected that the widow Kincaid had arranged the man's death. If they were happy together that's all that mattered.

Merriweather had now struck up a conversation with Eli and was looking to cut some of his costs by doing business with the Savannah Import/Export Company.

Maddy was now so big that she waddled when she walked. Cooper still had to sail to Antigua, but seeing how big she was, he said that he'd put the trip off.

"You will have time to go and return," Faith said, and Dagan agreed, so they sailed two days later on a Thursday.

At Cooper's request, Dagan sailed with him. Eli had been quick to give Cooper a letter delineating the monies expected for Cooper and his men.

When Dagan saw that he'd been included he smiled, "I put a bit away here and there."

"Aye, I saw that at times," Cooper replied.

The last night at sea before pulling into Antigua, Kate dined with Cooper and T. As the conversation slowed, Kate took a large swallow of her wine and then gave a sigh. "I want to thank all of you for taking me in at a bad time in my life. You allowed me to do the one thing I am good at, and that is help people. I'm not sure that I could have dealt with life like I have without you." She leaned way over so that she could reach Dagan's hand and gave it a squeeze. "Especially one ole salt. I've seen enough in the last year since we were taken, to be fully aware that nothing in life is guaranteed. If you want something you better grab it before it's gone. With that in mind, I've decided to marry Jake Anthony."

"That is good news, Kate," Cooper said.

"Well, you and T are taken, and Dagan turned me down," Kate joked. They all laughed then.

Dagan asked Kate, as they left Cooper's cabin, "Are you sure?"

"I'm sure," she replied.

Dagan kissed her on the forehead. "May God grant you a lifetime of love, health, and happiness."

That night secure in his cot, Dagan smiled. If they shared just a little of the things that he and Becky had, they would have a happy life.

✱✱✱

"Captain, repair on board," flew from the flagship. Expecting it, *Stag's* boat was in the water almost as soon as the signal was given. As they neared to the entry port, the challenge was made. The reply from Midshipman Shirreffs would be the last one for Cooper.

"*Stag*," the middy sang out, a tremble in his voice. Cooper grasped the boy's shoulder. He would miss the brave midshipman.

Quang had stayed on board *Stag*. He, Josiah, and House would shift Cooper's things to *SeaFire*. He'd be a passenger going home.

When Cooper's head reached level with the deck, the bosun's pipe shrilled out and the band played. Jake Anthony was there to greet him and, surprisingly, so was Admiral Davy. Hands were shaken and they all went to the admiral's cabin.

When the admiral had his back to them, Cooper handed a note to Jake. "From a lady," he whispered. Jake quickly slid the note under his waistband.

Refreshments were served and, when they sat down Cooper handed a wrapped package to Admiral Davy. He opened the package and took out a silk lace handkerchief and a green hat. The hat was round, with a bill completely around it and hanging from the bill was a green silk veil.

"That is all that is left of Calico, Admiral."

Admiral Davy sniffed the handkerchief. A perfumery smell still lingered. Cooper then opened a leather bag.

"Calico's ledgers, Admiral. They are sketchy in places, but overall not bad. They may bring closure to some of the missing ships."

"We've been able to piece together a fair number of those murdered," the admiral said by talking to survivors.

"We were able to rescue three more young girls. None were over twelve or thirteen as I recall. We were also able to rescue Merriweather Woodham's daughter, Kathleen."

"Good, good," Admiral Davy responded.

Cooper reached back into the bag and pulled out more. "This is my report and the master stated that you'd want to see the ship's logs. Finally, and I'm not sure who I should give this to, you or the governor. It is our clerk's letter of the monies that's due."

"I'll take it," Admiral Davy said. "You understand they'll try to wheedle you out of half of it." They all laughed but at the same time they knew the admiral's words were true.

***

T MADE IT TO Cooper's mother and Jean Paul's house within two hours after *Stag* dropped anchor. He'd knocked on the door but there was no answer. That was strange, he thought. He sat on the steps to the back entrance for a good half hour. He'd spotted a nice inn down the way and decided to walk there and get something to eat and drink. He'd just walked out on the street when a carriage passed.

Suddenly, much like it happened when this business first started, he heard his name shouted out and a figure was out of the carriage and running toward him. Only this time it was a woman—Dolcie.

***

AFTER A WEEK OF nonstop activity, Cooper was ready to throw his hands up. He'd been dined by the governor. The Westcoat children, Landis and Peter, were still staying with the Basnights. Letters had been written informing relatives of the tragic news of Sir Edward and Emma Westcoat. Landis and Peter had indicated their desire to remain on the island, rather than returning to England at that time. Was it fear of pirates? Cooper had taken the time to visit with the two of them. Peter's eyes were much better so the doctor felt that his eyes would fully heal with time. Cooper couldn't help but wonder if they would heal emotionally. He felt that it was important, so he told them that they had wiped out all the pirates.

"I'm glad," Peter said. "If you hadn't, I would have done it some way."

The last three days on Antigua were spent on his family's plantation. Things were improving as the main house was restored. The fence was replaced, and new houses for the workers were going up. His mother admitted that she never thought the place would be returned to the family.

She took Cooper for a short walk one morning. It was under a large tree that he saw his father's grave. "I thought that you should see this," his mother told him. "It shall be maintained from now on."

Cooper felt choked and had tears trickle down his cheeks.

"He'd be happy now, knowing the land is back in his family's possession," Cooper's mother said.

"Where it will stay," Cooper added.

EPILOGUE

DOLCIE AND T WERE married by the ship's captain, Johannes Ewers, the second day at sea after weighing anchor in Antigua. There would be a trip back to the island within a year. Cooper was to be the best man at Jake and Kate's wedding. Johannes had given the newlyweds the captain's cabin for the voyage back to Savannah.

"I wonder how they would sleep if they knew that there were two chests of gold beneath their cot," Johannes joked.

Dagan took three cigars out and passed one to each of his friends before lighting his own.

"It's been a long time since we first sailed together," Cooper said to Johannes.

"Aye, a lot of water has passed beneath the keel," Johannes responded.

"I finally feel relaxed," Cooper admitted to his friends.

"Enjoy it while you can," Dagan said. "When the little one comes along you'll find out that you would give anything to be back at sea."

Cooper smiled, "Maddy and Rosa have picked out a nurse for the baby."

"Bertha is her name, as I recall," Dagan said. "She was recommended by Rosa."

"She's got to be good if Rosa recommended her," Cooper replied.

Dagan nodded, "She said that she was young enough to grow old with Maddy."

Cooper didn't want to think about that. He and Maddy had hardly had time to live together. He didn't want to think about growing old. Not yet, anyway.

* * *

COOPER SENT WORD ASHORE via Quang when *SeaFire* dropped anchor in Savannah Harbor. The ship was soon wharfed up to the company's dock. A team of horses pulling a wagon came down to unload the chest of gold. Several armed guards were with them. Dagan rode along with Coop back up to the warehouse.

Cooper handed Eli a list of documents provided by the British for payments. A full decision had not been made on the recapture of the frigate HMS *Syren*. Cooper said to Eli, "The owners of the schooner named the *Blue Caribee* would also like to make a direct offer for the return of the schooner."

It had not been brought up, but Cooper had been made aware of a ten gun sloop that Calico used as his own. It was not found at Deadman Bay. Being of the mind that the less said is often the best said, the ship was never mentioned in Cooper's report.

Once they were at the warehouse, Cooper borrowed Eli's buggy. He, Dagan, and Quang were going home. T would get a room for Dolcie and himself. Cooper would meet with him the next day as the crew gathered. After everyone was paid, Eli would take T and Dolcie to look at a farm that was for sale about fifteen miles north, just below the South Carolina border.

The homecoming was all that Cooper expected it to be. "It is over now," Maddy said, more a question that a statement.

"It's over, Maddy. I can now be lazy, watch the crops grow and we can have fat babies," Cooper replied.

Maddy kissed her husband passionately. "I knew this day would come, Sir Pirate."

Gabe rolled his eyes as Faith squeezed her husband's hand. Dagan stole a piece of cornbread and slid out the kitchen door. He felt tired, and as he sat in his chair with his feet propped up, Priscilla came in.

"Mr. Dagan," she squealed. Rushing over she gave him a big hug. "I'm so glad to see you back. My, it's drafty in here. Let me build you a little fire."

✱✱✱

"COOPER…HUH! COOPER.,."

"What!" he asked.

"Get up," Maddy replied.

"Why?"

"I think that it's time," she said.

"Time for what?"

"To pop out this baby that you filled my belly with."

Cooper was up instantly. He slid on his britches, grabbed a shirt and ran to wake Faith. He then woke Rosa, and said "Go wake Quang and have him bring the doctor."

Quang woke up, hearing Cooper's voice, and had Luke hook up the carriage. By the time Quang left, every candle and lantern in the house was lit. Smiling to himself, Dagan got up. Rosa woke Priscilla and had her get Brand up to go get Bertha.

Cooper was pacing the floor thirty minutes later. *Where were Quang and the doctor? Thank goodness Bertha had just gotten there.* The sun was just rising when Quang pulled up with a frightened looking doctor.

"Quang's driving scare you?" Luke asked, as he helped the doctor down.

"No, it was his hands around my throat and him saying hurry up or I'd never see another day. Missy needs you now." Coop had said to go get him and don't come back without him.

The doctor had the smell of a lingering brandy on his breath. *He seemed sober enough to deliver a baby*, Luke thought, so maybe Quang had sobered the man up.

Cooper paced the floor between the sitting room and the kitchen. The wall clock struck midnight. Cooper checked his watch and looked at the calendar. It was November 13th.

Inside the bedroom, he could hear voices speaking loudly, "Push, push." He could hear Maddy scream. Damn, he could use a drink, and then it grew quiet. It was so hushed that Cooper started to worry, and then he heard a baby cry. Everyone was smiling now. Gabe was shaking his hand and Dagan was pounding his back.

After a minute, the doctor stepped out. "Congratulations, sir, you have a fine son."

Gabe was passing out cigars when Bertha burst out of the bedroom. She grabbed the doctor's arm and jerked him back into the bedroom.

Fear gripped Cooper. He didn't know what to do. Were Maddy and the baby alright? He reached for the brandy bottle and poured some in a glass, downing it in one gulp. He could feel the burning as the liquid went down.

The baby was crying again, thank God. The door opened again and the doctor walked out smiling. "As I was saying a while ago, you have a fine son...and a beautiful daughter."

Cooper stood there with a blank look on his face, a son and daughter. He was lost as everyone began to celebrate. He went in to see Maddy a few minutes later.

"I guess that I shouldn't have expected anything different when I let a pirate have his way with me. It's no wonder my belly was so big."

"You enjoyed every minute of it, you wench." He kissed Maddy then.

When he pulled back, she whispered, "Yes I did and if I was able I'd show you just how much." Cooper smiled at her.

"Coop!"

"Yes," Cooper replied.

"Won't Jessie and Josie be surprised," Maddy said.

Bertha walked in then, "It's time that you let her rest."

Cooper nodded. "Do we need to get someone to help?" he asked Bertha.

"No, suh, I can handle them two and two more next time."

Cooper shook his head and gave a sigh as he walked out. *I don't know if I could.*

HISTORICAL NOTES

AT THE END OF the War of 1812, hundreds of privateers sailed the Caribbean preying on enemy shipping. The Peace Treaty thought by most to be a godsend had the opposite affect for the privateers. The privateersmen now found themselves on the beach with no livelihood. Therefore, a good many returned to their old ways of raiding ships, only with no Letter of Marque to support them, they became pirates.

With the War at an end, Caribbean and American shipping lanes were full of merchant vessels with valuable cargoes. These ships became easy pickings for the pirates.

Because of the heavy losses, both British and American forces worked together to battle the rogues raiding the shipping lanes.

Public outcry got so bad that in 1821, U.S. President Monroe authorized the establishment of an Anti-pirate Squadron. It was placed under the command of Commodore David Porter. Porter was assigned sixteen ships to combat the pirates. The ships were small, had shallow drafts and were fast sailors. One ship was an early paddle steamer.

Because the ships were all small, they were called the Mosquito Fleet. The fleet was based at Key West, Florida; then known as Thompson's Island.

The defeat of the Cuban pirate, Diabolito (Little Devil) was one of the fleet's biggest captures.

Deadman Bay Historical Marker – Some years ago I was on a fishing trip with several friends. We stopped for gas and cokes and I saw the sign or historical marker. It impressed me enough that years later when putting together my story for The Hunter, the sign and name, Deadman Bay came back to me. Steinhatchee is a small fishing town. You can see the bay from where you park. The falls are eight miles up the river and are now a recreational area. It's worth an overnight trip to visit the area.

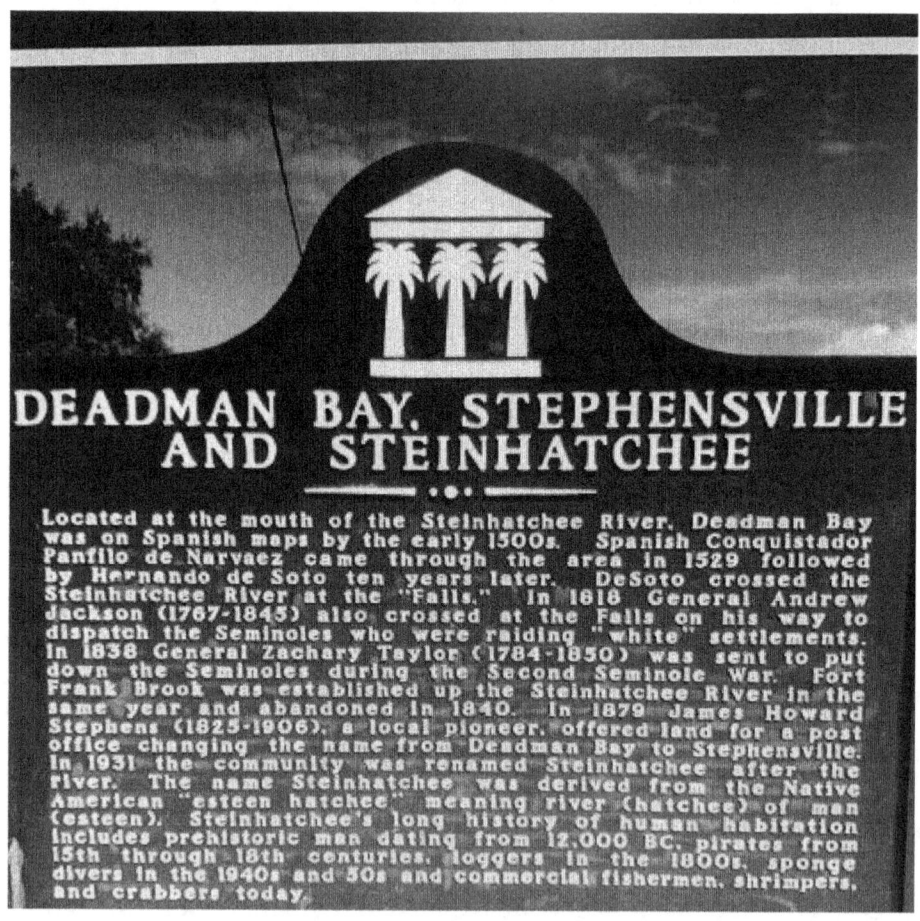

DEADMAN BAY, STEPHENSVILLE AND STEINHATCHEE

Located at the mouth of the Steinhatchee River, Deadman Bay was on Spanish maps by the early 1500s. Spanish Conquistador Panfilo de Narvaez came through the area in 1529 followed by Hernando de Soto ten years later. DeSoto crossed the Steinhatchee River at the "Falls." In 1818 General Andrew Jackson (1767-1845) also crossed at the Falls on his way to dispatch the Seminoles who were raiding "white" settlements. In 1838 General Zachary Taylor (1784-1850) was sent to put down the Seminoles during the Second Seminole War. Fort Frank Brook was established up the Steinhatchee River in the same year and abandoned in 1840. In 1879 James Howard Stephens (1825-1906), a local pioneer, offered land for a post office changing the name from Deadman Bay to Stephensville. In 1931 the community was renamed Steinhatchee after the river. The name Steinhatchee was derived from the Native American "esteen hatchee" meaning river (hatchee) of man (esteen). Steinhatchee's long history of human habitation includes prehistoric man dating from 12,000 BC, pirates from 15th through 18th centuries, loggers in the 1800s, sponge divers in the 1940s and 50s and commercial fishermen, shrimpers, and crabbers today.